FLIRTING WITH THE FRENEMY

PIPPA GRANT

ONE

Ellie Ryder, aka a woman in need of more than ice cream to fill the hole in her heart

WHEN I RULE THE WORLD, peppermint crunch ice cream will be available all year long, because assholes who break people's hearts don't restrict their assholery and heart-breaking to Christmas.

Unless, apparently, they're *my* asshole.

Check that.

My *former* asshole.

I stab my spoon straight into the cold carton that I grabbed at the store on the way here and ignore the twinkling holiday cheer on my parents' gigantic tree in the living room. It's late, so I didn't tell them I was coming over, but I don't want to spend one more night at my house this week.

Alone.

Sleeping in the bed where Patrick screwed me—and then screwed me over—just two nights ago.

Merry Christmas, Ellie. I'm in love with my neighbor.

I leave them a note taped to the coffee pot to let them know I'm here, then stomp down the stairs—softly, so I don't wake them—and turn the corner into the rec room, where I pound the light switch up.

And then almost scream.

There's a lump of a man sprawled on the couch watching a black-and-white movie, and as soon as the lights go on, he winces and throws his arm over his eyes. "*Christ*," he snarls.

My heart backpedals from the precipice where it was about to leap, then surges into a furious beat all over again. "What the fuck are you doing here?"

Wyatt Morgan drops his arm and squints at me. "Oh, good. It's Ellie. Drop in to rub some salt in the wound?"

I inhale another bite of ice cream while I glare at him, because I didn't ask *him* to be here, and he's scowling just as hard as I'm glaring. "Beck's place is downtown. Go get drunk there." Even as the words leave my mouth, guilt stabs me in the lung.

Not the heart, because first, I'd have to *like* my brother's best friend for my heart to be affected, and second, because I'm not sure I have a heart left.

I'm in a shit-tastic mood—who dumps their girlfriend *on Christmas Eve?*—but even in the midst of my own pity party, I know why Wyatt's sitting in my parents' basement, stewing himself in beer and watching *It's a Wonderful Life*.

He doesn't even roll his eyes at my order to get out.

"Beck's having a party," he informs me. "Didn't want to go. Guess you weren't invited. Or you prefer to add to the shit pile here."

He tips back his beer, and another guilt knife attacks me, this time in the liver.

It's entirely possible he has bigger problems than I do. I lost a boyfriend that I'll probably acknowledge soon enough—for real, not just in a fit of anger—that I'm better off without.

The courts just handed Wyatt a final divorce decree that means he only gets to see his kid once a month.

If he travels five hundred miles to do it every time.

"Shove it, Morgan," I tell him. "I don't kick a man when he's down."

"Since when?"

"Oh, please. Like you can talk."

It's been like this since we were kids. My brother's childhood best friend is the only man in the entire universe who can get under my skin and bring out my ugly faster than you can blink, and I swear he takes joy in doing it.

A ninety-five on your math test, Ellie? Why not perfect?

Nice shot, but you're still down by eight.

Who taught you to hold a pool cue, a blind monkey?

And damn if all that taunting didn't make me try harder every fucking time.

Because when he wasn't taunting me, he was the first one holding out a hand to pull me off the pavement or out of the mud when I inevitably got trampled trying to keep up with Beck and his friends in soccer, street hockey, basketball, and whatever else I swore I was big enough to do with them.

He eyeballs my breasts, and my whole body lights up like the Christmas lights all over downtown.

"You gonna eat that whole carton?" he asks, and *fuck*, he's not looking at my chest.

He's looking at my ice cream, and here I am, getting turned on at the idea that he's finally noticed I'm a woman.

I have issues.

So many fucking issues.

I fling myself onto the couch next to him. "It's loser ice cream, so yeah, I am," I grumble. "Here. Have a bite, you drunk asshole."

Those gray eyes connect with mine, and *dammit*, that's straight lust pooling in my belly.

He's sporting a thick five-o'clock shadow, and even sprawled out on the worn flowery couch in my parents' basement, he exudes power and masculinity in a way I never would've expected from the skinny pipsqueak peeking out from behind his grandmother's legs on the front porch twenty-some years ago.

Or maybe it's the tight black T-shirt, with his biceps testing the limits of the cotton and detailing his trim stomach, even sitting down, and the gray sweatpants hinting at a more substantial package than I ever would've given him credit for.

Plus the knowledge that Pipsqueak Wyatt grew up to join the Air Force as some kind of badass pilot who flies untested aircraft, which takes a hell of a lot of guts, if you ask me when I'm willing to admit something like that about him.

Which is apparently tonight.

You used to like him, my subconscious reminds me, because it's forgetting its place.

I'd tell it to shut up, that I don't go for guys who don't appreciate me, except isn't that what I just spent the last two years of my life doing?

He reaches for my spoon, and our fingers brush when he takes it. A shiver ripples over my skin. I look away to watch the movie while I hold the carton for him to dig out a scoopful.

George Bailey is arguing with Mr. Potter on the TV, and I can feel the heat off Wyatt's skin penetrating my baggy Ryder Consulting sweatshirt.

I snort softly to myself.

Of course he wasn't staring at my chest. He can't even see it under this thing.

You're holding the basketball wrong, Ellie.

It went in, didn't it?

Yeah, but you could be more consistent if you worked on your form.

Damn him for sneaking into my head. Damn him for taunting me.

Damn him for being right.

Because I did work on my fucking form, and Beck—who's three years older than I am—quit playing ball with me after I beat him in a free throw contest when I was twelve.

He said it was because he was *working on other stuff with the guys,* but I knew my brother better than that.

I *knew* he quit playing with me because I beat him.

Wyatt still took the challenge though. He'd tell me I got lucky when I won. He'd tell me what I did wrong when I didn't.

And I worked my ass off getting better and better until I beat him *every time.*

And then he lost interest too.

I take the spoon from him and grunt softly while I dig deeper into the carton. "You were such an asshole when we were kids."

He grunts back and snags the spoon again. "*You* were such an asshole when we were kids."

"You were just insecure about getting your ass beat by a girl on the basketball court."

"You just hated that you wouldn't have been half as good without me."

I take my spoon back and shovel in. My extra-large bite of ice cream makes my brain cramp, but fuck if I'll let him see me hurt.

Not that I can hide it. I know my face is blotchy from crying before I drove over here, and my eyes are that special kind of dry that comes after too many tears.

I can count on one hand the number of times I've talked to him solo since he and Beck and the guys graduated high school. He's changed. His voice is deeper, if that's possible. His body definitely harder—*god*, those biceps, and his forearms are tight, with large veins snaking over the corded muscle from his elbows to his knuckles—his square jaw more chiseled, his eyes steel rather than simple gray.

And it's not like he lost custody of his kid because he's an asshole.

Beck was blabbering all about it at Christmas dinner yesterday. *Dude got so fucked. The military gave him orders here, so Lydia moved first, with Tucker. She hated military life. But then his orders got changed last-minute so he ended up in Georgia, she filed for divorce, and he's been fighting the military and the courts ever since to get back to where he can be closer to his kid. He's in fucking hell right now. And if he cuts bait on the military, they'll toss him in jail for being AWOL. He's fucked. He's SO fucked.*

There goes George Bailey, leaving Mr. Potter's office to go get drunk.

Wyatt tips back his beer. A holiday brew. Like that can take away the misery of hurting this time of year. I don't know why he's here instead of taking advantage of every last minute with his kid, but then, I don't know much about divorce either.

Maybe this isn't his Christmas to see his son. Maybe Lydia's being an asshole.

One more bottle sits on the end table next to him, but just one.

Drowning his sorrows with a broken George Bailey.

"I'm sorry about your shitty divorce," I say.

Sullenly.

Just in case he thinks I might have a twinge of sympathy for him. That won't do for either of us.

He sets the bottle down and grabs the spoon again.

"So you're sharing because you feel sorry for me."

"Maybe I'm sharing because I'm not a total asshole."

"But I still am?"

I heave a sigh. I don't want to be sitting here with Wyatt Morgan any more than I want to give in to the urge to go running over to Patrick's swanky condo in the Warehouse district and beg him to give us another chance.

I was supposed to be getting engaged this Christmas.

Not dumped.

And I can't tell if that searing pain in my chest is my heart or my pride.

Or both.

Probably both.

It's not like the sex was even *good* the other night, and he rolled over and checked his email right after, so logically, I know I'm not missing anything.

But my fucking heart still hurts.

"Misery loves company more than it cares what the company is," I tell Wyatt.

He looks at me while he shoves the spoon back in the carton, then waves a hand in a circle, gesturing to me. "*This* is you being miserable?"

"I know, I make it look good."

"I thought you looked like this all the time."

"Asshole."

He smirks, but it's a dark smirk. Like he *wanted* me to call him an asshole, but it didn't make him feel as good as he hoped it would. "What the hell do you have to be miserable about?"

"I broke a nail."

He snags my hand and lifts it, turning it to inspect my perfectly trimmed, newly manicured nails, and tremors skittle out from the point where his thumb rests inside my palm.

It's like he's turning me on.

Patrick hasn't turned me on in *months*. That's what's supposed to happen, right? You settle down with one person and get yourself into a rut and the sex becomes routine instead of exciting. It's normal, right?

Or you were an idiot who should've dumped him a year ago, my subconscious helpfully offers.

I snatch my hand back, but I'm still ridiculously aware of Wyatt beside me.

The hitch in his breath.

The subtle scent of cinnamon and beer wafting off him.

The way his gaze is still trained on me. "So you got dumped too," he muses.

"Shut. Up."

That would've been more effective if I'd been able to say it without dribbling peppermint crunch ice cream down my chin and my voice wobbling.

He reaches out and wipes the drip off my chin, and I realize he's leaning into my space.

My heart's pounding. My breasts are getting full and heavy. My mouth is going dry, even with ice cream still lingering on my tongue, and I almost choke when I swallow.

"Merry fucking Christmas to us," he says. His nose is inches from mine, and his lids are lowering over darkened eyes.

"There's no *fucking* going on," I point out, my breath getting shallower as I glance down his just-barely-off-center nose to his stupidly perfect lips.

"There's not, is there?" he muses while his gaze darts to my lips too. "There's only getting fucked over."

Every time he says *fuck*, I get a shot of heat between my legs.

"You're in my bubble," I whisper.

"Maybe I'm trying to annoy you to make myself feel better."

"Maybe if you wanted to annoy me, you should take your clothes off."

Holy shit, I just said that.

He holds my gaze for half a second, and then his shirt goes flying. He settles back against the couch, still leaning into my space, but now with acres and acres of hard chest and sculpted stomach and cut hips and that perfect trail of hair arrowing down to disappear under his sweatpants.

"Now, what are you going to do to annoy me?" he asks.

I *should* dump this carton of ice cream on his head.

But I *want* to do something else.

Something wrong.

But right? Maybe?

Fuck it.

Thinking's what got me in trouble with Patrick. I *thought* he was what I wanted. I *thought* I loved him because I *thought* I should. I *thought* he'd be a good partner. I *thought* we wanted the same things in life.

I *thought* Wyatt was annoying.

But my body isn't thinking.

My body just *wants*.

I slap the ice cream onto the wobbly end table that my brother broke years ago, and then I peel off my sweatshirt and the stained college T-shirt beneath it.

"Annoyed yet?" I purr.

Oh, fuck, I'm *purring*.

His gaze dips to my chest, and his sweatpants tent.

Holy hell.

Wyatt Morgan is packing, and it's making my clit tingle.

That hasn't happened just by *looking* at a man in months.

"Yeah," he says, his voice thick and low. "Yeah, I'm fucking annoyed."

I rise and shimmy out of my leggings, because this is a bad idea, but every *good* idea I've ever had hasn't gotten me what I wanted in life, has it?

"Christ, Ellie," he rasps out.

"You only wish you looked this good," I tell him, but I can't keep my voice steady either.

I'd blame the ice cream for the heady tingling in my fingers and toes, but my blood's not spiked with anything more than sugar.

I let Wyatt take his time looking at me, because I *know* I look good. I hit the gym for weights four mornings a week. I run marathons. I still have curves. I don't run without a heavy-duty sports bra and my ass could squash a supermodel, but I won't apologize for being built like a woman.

I *am* a woman. A strong, powerful, unique woman who fucking deserves exactly what I'm seeing in the raw desire in Wyatt's gray eyes.

If he's never noticed my body before, he's noticing now.

"You need to put your clothes back on," he says, but his eyes aren't in agreement with his words.

His eyes are offering to use my body to make my brain forget what my heart's suffering.

"Or what?" I ask.

He visibly swallows, but he doesn't answer.

He doesn't look away either.

I slip one bra strap down my shoulder, letting it hang in the crook of my elbow, not off, but not on either.

"Ellie," he warns, his hand going to his pants over his cock, like he can't decide if he wants to press it down to stop it, or if he wants to jerk himself off while he watches me strip.

"You're hurting," I say, slipping my other bra strap halfway down my arm too. I'm still covered by my simple satin demicups, but I reach behind me like I'm going to unhook the band, and we both know he'll be getting an eyeful of my breasts if I do it. "I'm hurting. I don't want to hurt. Do you?"

"No," he rasps out.

"Don't you want to just say *fuck them* and feel good for a few minutes?"

"Yes."

I shut down all the warning signals alarming inside my head, because they're not all *don't screw your brother's best friend*.

Some of them are *you know how long it took to forget him the last time you got a crush on him*.

And some *he's unavailable, dumbass, and so are you. You know you can't do this without feelings getting involved*.

Can't I?

"You're probably a terrible lay," I say as I drop my bra.

He rises, and his pants hit the ground.

So do his boxers.

I take in the sight of his cock bobbing and straining, and I have to physically stop myself from reaching for it.

He's long. Thick. With a blunt head and dark curls framing his balls, so unlike Patrick's total blondness.

"You probably lay there like a cold limp noodle," he says.

"Try me."

He's suddenly crushing his mouth against mine, and he tastes like cinnamon and beer and summer, and his skin is hot against mine, his tongue unforgiving, his cock hard against my belly while his hands roam up my sides to tease the underside of my breasts.

I moan into his mouth. He groans in response. Our tongues clash, an inevitable extension of the war we've always waged since before we were old enough to understand it. I scrape his back with my nails. He squeezes my breasts. I push his shoulders until he's on his knees, following him all the way down to the ground.

This is insane.

I should stop.

"Condom," he sputters. "Wallet."

I grab it off the end table. "Hurry up before I change my mind."

He stills.

Like he's changing *his* mind.

So I grab his cock and pump it in my fist before he can tell me no.

I don't want to *think*.

I just want to *feel*.

And right now, my skin is on fire, my pussy is aching, and my breasts are heavy and desperate for attention.

"Fuck, Ellie," he groans, his head dropping back while he fumbles for the condom.

As soon as he's pulled it out of his wallet, I snag it and tear it open. "Touch my breasts," I order.

"Christ, so soft," he mutters while he tests the weight of my D-cups and teases my nipples.

Every brush of his thumb over one of my tips sends a shock-wave of desire straight to my core. He alternates. One nipple.

Then the other. Like my body is an instrument, and he's teasing new notes of arousal to the surface.

"So hard," I mutter back while I roll the condom down his steel shaft.

I cup his balls, and the next thing I know, he's rolled me onto my back, his mouth sealing over mine again. We fumble together to yank my panties off. I part my legs and arch into him, and he pushes into me.

It's new. And weird.

But not unwelcome.

He fills me, sliding easily into my soaking heat even as he stretches my inner walls, and I tilt my hips to take him as deep as I can.

"You drive me fucking insane," he rasps as he pumps into me.

I don't answer, because *oh, fuck*. "There. Right there." I buck my hips, the tension building high and tight right in that deepest part of me that he hits every time he thrusts in.

"Don't close your eyes," he orders.

Against my will, I open them.

He's watching my face while he hammers inside, faster and deeper, watching me gasp in pleasure while he fills me to the hilt and pulls back just long enough to make it that much better when he strokes deep inside me with the next thrust.

How long have I hated Wyatt Morgan?

And how long have I possibly just been *afraid*?

Told you so, my subconscious whispers, but he hits that sweet spot deep inside me again, and I come completely undone. My orgasm roars out of me, squeezing and pulsing and spasming around his hard cock, a silent cry on my lips while he groans and strains, holding himself inside me while he grits his teeth, eyes still penetrating mine, anger simmering, pain simmering, *release* simmering.

The two of us are quite the pair.

And it's not nearly as terrifying a thought as it should be.

I'm panting, my breath loud in my own ears, when he suddenly freezes.

"Oh, shit," he whispers. He pushes up to his knees, pulling

out so quickly and covering the goods so fast that my vagina almost gets whiplash. "Fuck. Ellie." He shakes his head, gaze darting in a panic around the room. "We shouldn't have done that."

The words take a minute to sink in.

And he takes advantage of my dumbfounded silence to hop back into his clothes. "Fuck. Sorry. I—"

"Shut up." I lunge for my own clothes. Tears are flooding my sinuses, and they'll be leaking out my eyeballs in approximately two seconds if I don't get myself under control. "Just shut up."

I dive for my clothes too.

"Ellie—"

"*Shut. Up.*"

That sympathy. That regret. That *this was a mistake.* It's all in the two syllables of my name on his lips.

Fuck. *Fuck.*

He moves toward me, but I shove him in the chest until he backs off.

He's right, of course.

It's Wyatt.

He's always right. If this was a mistake, if *I'm* a mistake, then yeah, clearly I'm a mistake.

A mistake who thought that screwing her brother's best friend was the solution to heartbreak.

I don't look at him while I dash for the door.

"*Ellie,*" he calls in a hushed whisper, but I ignore him.

I've already been someone's *mistake* recently.

And as I barrel into the cold winter night and throw myself into the car, I vow to myself that I'll never be *anyone*'s mistake *ever* again.

"Never again," I whisper as I start my car.

"Never again," I whisper as I gun it on the way down my parents' street.

"Never again," I'm whispering through tears five minutes later on the I-256 loop.

I see the movement flying up the entrance ramp next to me a second too late.

There's a flash, sparks, a crack, a jolt.

Spinning.
Crunching.
Glass shattering.
Metal buckling.
Pain.
Blinding hot pain.
Never again.
It's my last thought before everything goes black.

TWO

Six months later...

WYATT MORGAN, aka a single dad military man unaware that an unresolved piece of his past is lurking in the bathtub

THE HOUSE IS TOO QUIET.

Probably because Tucker quit talking as soon as he saw the socks and bra hanging on the chandelier in the foyer. I give myself a mental pat on the back.

Way to go, Dad. Introduce him to party central at a young age.

If Beck Ryder wasn't the closest thing I had to a brother, and if just being here didn't already bring back the same lingering guilt that's been with me the last six months, I'd be plotting to put Icy Hot in those briefs he models right about now.

Instead, I give the living room a cursory glance and stifle a sigh while I kick my sandals off on the entry mat and nudge Tucker to do the same. Books, magazines, robot toys, and empty mugs and glasses are scattered over every flat surface of the spacious living space, from the end tables to the wide-plank maple floor. The mess ruins the effect of the tall bay windows overlooking the spruce and oaks sloping down the side of the mountain to the little landlocked town of Shipwreck, Virginia in the valley below.

A subtle scent of wood smoke hangs in the air, and the massive stone fireplace separating the living room from the dining room needs the ashes cleaned out. The kitchen is just as much a disaster, with dirty plates, cups, mixing bowls, and pots and pans scattered all about.

Use my weekend house, Beck said. *Somebody should*.

Go clean my weekend house, he meant.

He needs to be more careful with who he lets in here when he's gone.

A family picture on the mantle catches my eye, and I do my best not to wince.

The guilt is still there. The guilt, and the lie.

I pissed her off.

That's all I told Beck about what happened before Ellie's accident.

Of course you did, Levi had said, because he'd also been lurking at the hospital when I showed up to check on her as soon as I got Beck's text the next day. I'd never been so glad to have a buffer, and felt less like I deserved one, and after what I grew up with before my mom finally moved us to Copper Valley, that's saying something. Levi hadn't cracked a grin when he'd added, *Pissing off Ellie is what you do.*

Fuck, man, you got your own problems, Beck had told me. *Don't put this on yourself too.*

And just like that, I was forgiven.

By them, anyway.

Not by *her* though.

And not by me.

It's gotten easier to get back in the groove of participating in the group texts with all the guys from the neighborhood, but being here, in Beck's second—third? fourth?—home, surrounded by reminders of his sister, makes me tenser than I've been in months.

Coming here was a bad idea.

But I'm not here for me.

Not entirely.

I squeeze Tucker's shoulder. His gaze has drifted from the chandelier to the life-size cardboard cutout of Beck in his skivvies standing in the corner.

The air-brushing on that thing would be hilarious if my son wasn't gaping at Beck's six-pack. I turn the thing around, then nod toward the hallway beyond the kitchen. "C'mon, little dude. Let's go find the bedrooms."

He nods back. Sort of. I guide him past the kitchen and down the hallway toward the two bedrooms on this level. His suitcase goes into the guest bedroom, and I'm about to fling my duffel inside the master, but the rumpled sheets on the king-size four-poster bed, the glass of water on the heavy nightstand, the open suitcase next to the stone fireplace stuffed with—*parrots?*—and the flowery scent tickling my nose give me pause.

But it's the soft light flickering in the bathroom doorway that makes the hairs on the back of my neck stand up.

I put a hand out to stop Tucker from coming closer. "Stay here," I murmur, my pulse suddenly hammering.

Since Christmas, it's been just me. Alone. Except the one weekend a month I've flown to Copper Valley to visit my son.

Checking out an intruder? Twenty-eight days a month, I can handle that.

But on the first day I get Tucker for the summer? When it's not just *my* neck on the line?

This is *not* how our week of vacation is supposed to go.

I slide my phone out of my pocket and creep softly to the bathroom door, one hand held back to remind Tucker to stay and be quiet.

He's seven.

This isn't going to end well.

But just as I decide getting the hell out of here and calling a sheriff is probably a better idea, I see what's lurking in the bathroom.

A woman.

Alone.

In the corner tub.

Her dark hair is piled in a short ponytail on top of her head.

The faint sound of country music drifts out of her earbuds. Candles line the tub shelf and the platform it sits on, causing the flickering glow. The bath bubbles are so high I can't see her face.

My heart gives a squeeze and shoots out guilt, but I tell it to knock it off.

Beck lets anybody who asks use this house.

It's not Ellie.

Her hair's too short and too dark. Ellie always has blond streaks in her hair.

I step onto the cool tile floor, and I'm about to clear my throat to get her attention when Tucker exclaims, "A bubble bath!"

The woman shrieks, straightens, and spins, wide blue eyes connecting with mine for a split second before she disappears.

One second, she's gape-mouthed and goggling like she's just as shocked to see us as we are to see her, and the next, there's a splash that sets my heart spiraling into a panic, because *fuck me*, that's Ellie.

A flurry of foamy bubbles shoots into the air as she goes under the water. Her arm flaps up, then the other, waving wildly like she's trying to find purchase to pull herself up. I dash across the slick tile to grab for her in the deep tub. My hand connects with soft wet flesh, and suddenly I'm getting a fist to the chest as she breaks through the water. "Back up, asshole. I'll fucking cut you!"

Fuck, that voice.

It's coming out of a face covered with bubbles from the top of her head to the foam sticking to her eyelashes all the way down to the droopy bubble beard, but I know that voice, and it has my pounding heart suddenly beating from somewhere around my voice box.

"Ellie. Are you—"

The bubble eyes blink. "*Wyatt*?"

The shriek is amplified by the hard surfaces in the bathroom, bouncing off the glass window over the tub, the mirror, the hard floor.

She gasps, looks down and flings her arms over her bubble-covered chest, and ducks back down, but then she shrieks and disappears under the water again, arms flailing again, and what the *fuck* is she soaking in that's making the tub so slippery?

I bend at the waist to reach into the tub and grab onto her arm and pull, but no sooner does she surface than her eyes narrow. "Let. Go," she sputters around the bubbles cascading down her face.

"So you can drown?" Christ, she nearly died the last time I saw her. I'm not letting her drown.

No matter how much she irritates the fuck out of me.

Or how—

Nope.

Not thinking about Ellie in any other way than the *annoying* and *alive* ways.

Still, we're so close, I can count the specks of midnight in her blue irises and the new list of reasons she has to hate me.

And I know she's naked under those bubbles.

Fuck fuck *fuck. Think about my kid. Remember Beck. Think about Beck in his underwear...*

Her eyelids snap up and down, more heat—*anger*, not interest —surging out of them. "I'm not going to—fu—"

Her words are cut off as she slips and flails again. She doesn't go under, because she grabs a handful of my shirt.

And pulls.

Hard.

The floor slips beneath me, and suddenly *I'm* falling face-first into the bubbles.

Wet heat crashes over my face and soaks into my T-shirt. I choke on a lungful of soapy water and come up sputtering.

I probably deserve that.

And more.

"What the fu—he—heck was that for?" I spit out around a cough while I shove away from the tub though, because while I can admit to myself that I deserved that, I'm not ready to admit it to her.

I'm still pissed at her for ignoring me so effectively for the past six months.

She huddles in a corner, firmly gripping the faucet. "Get out."

"Dad, you got bubbles on your head," Tucker laughs. "Can I have bubbles? Can I take your picture?"

The force of Ellie's glare is so hot I'm surprised the bubbles don't melt. "Get. Out," she repeats.

I swipe water off my face and ignore the stinging in my eyes. "Gladly. You're welcome for trying to help."

She flips me the bird.

Not the first time.

Won't be the last.

Ellie Ryder and me?

We mix as well as water and lava.

And I don't want to talk about how fucking good it feels to finally confirm for myself that she's still in one piece.

That she's still breathing.

And that she still hates me.

More so, if that was possible.

I hate that she hates me, but I also need her to hate me.

Fuck, we're complicated.

"Can I take a bubble bath?" Tucker wants to know while I pull him back out of the bedroom, grabbing my duffel and then his suitcase from the guest bedroom too. Water sloshes off my shirt and drips onto the runner while we head for the stairs.

Fucking Beck.

He knew.

He knew she'd be here.

Dude, seriously, get the stick out of your ass, fuck your pride, and use my place out in Shipwreck. Tucker will love the pirate festival, and you're not gonna get a more comfortable bed. Or a better chance to teach him to play Pac-Man. Or a cheaper vacation. How much are you paying in alimony? Fuck.

"That was funny, Dad. You were taking a bubble bath with a girl. Mom says I'm too old to take baths with anyone, but you're way older than me, and you were doing it. Can we take a bubble bath together? I won't tell Mom. Promise."

My heart trips again, but this time, it's an entirely different reason.

How much does he promise his mother he won't tell me?

He's already grown an inch and a half since I saw him for two short days last month.

What else am I missing?

Forget Ellie.

Beck's not lying about how well she's healing. She'll be fine, and she can hate me all she wants.

Tucker's the only thing I need to concentrate on for the next week while I'm on leave. And then every spare minute the rest of the summer until I have to bring him back to his mom.

"Yeah, bud. Let's go see if there's a big tub upstairs."

Hopefully Ellie will clear out by morning.

But even if she doesn't, we can avoid her. House is big, and we have tons to do in Shipwreck.

She might've invaded this house, but she won't interfere with my vacation with my son.

Unless she needs me.

Not that she'd ever admit it.

And not that I want to admit it either.

I scrub a hand over my face as we step into the first bedroom on the second floor. The queen bed is decked out with a comforter featuring Beck making moon-eyes in his briefs, and the pillow shams are printed with matching pictures of him winking.

Crazy fucker.

"Dad? Why's your friend's picture all over everywhere? And why's he naked?" Tucker asks.

This is going to be one long week.

THREE

Ellie

MY DOODLE PAD.

I left my doodle pad in the living room.

Where Wyatt Morgan is headed *with his son.*

I yank my dripping phone out of the water—*wonderful*—and hoist myself onto the edge of the tub, stifling a groan at the ache radiating from my left hip to my knee. The scars aren't red and angry anymore, but they're still ugly and twisted, and I still can't move as fast as I used to.

Especially not after slipping in the tub three fucking times. So the answer would be *yes*, I still need that stupid anti-slip mat.

Dammit.

After I wipe the worst of the bubbles off my face, I do my best not to limp over the towels that I toss on the ground to prevent me from slipping on the slick tile floor. The air's cold now, but my bathrobe is warm, thanks to Beck's towel warmer.

Once I have my slippers on—simple granny slippers with, you guessed it, grippy foot pads on the bottom—and my phone in my robe pocket, I carefully creak open the bedroom door.

There are voices, but they sound like they're coming from upstairs.

It takes me longer than it should to get to the kitchen, dig out a box of Rice-a-Roni—no, my brother apparently *doesn't* keep plain rice here—and get my phone drying out as best I can.

And then I go in search of my doodle pad.

It's not on the glass end tables, in any of the magazine piles, or tucked into the crocheted ivory afghan on the brown leather couch. Nor is it between the couch cushions or hidden in the recliners. Not in the papers and random old mail on the coffee table, or on the fireplace hearth.

I look at the stack of magazines again, my blood pressure starting to rise.

No one gets to see my doodle pad.

Especially anyone under eighteen.

Or possibly thirty.

Or with a penis.

Or who *creeps up on me in the bathtub*.

My brother is getting an earful as soon as my phone's dry.

I was doodling out here this afternoon after unloading my car, which I probably should've let Monica help me with, but it's her wedding week, and I'm her maid of honor, dammit, not her friend who needs babysitting. I sat in *that* recliner, swiveled it to face the scenery, and drew—

Never mind what I drew.

The point is, I distinctly remember setting my doodle pad *right there* on the end table.

And it's *gone*.

Nothing else is missing.

Just my doodle pad.

A shriek of laughter from above makes me eyeball the stairs. I could go ask Wyatt where he put it.

Or be polite and ask if he's *seen* it. The tones of his voice carry through the ceiling as well, low, deep, and carefully modulated, because that's Wyatt for you.

Always calm.

Always in control.

Always fucking *right*.

Even about mistakes. *Oh, fuck, Ellie, we shouldn't have done that.*

I shake my head, because the two things I absolutely will *not* think about are Wyatt's hot, sweaty, naked body on mine, and the sound of metal crunching on metal and glass at sixty miles an hour in the dark.

Fuck.

Fuck.

Now I'm thinking about it.

About the dark. And the cold. And the pain.

The chill starts in my left femur and spreads a shiver through my bladder and up into that spot right beneath the bottom of my breastbone. The scent of blood floods my sinuses. My vision narrows, my skin goes clammy, and I get that itch between my shoulder blades while my lungs shrink to the size of a walnut.

I'm drowning.

I'm drowning in hot metal and sharp glass and snowflakes.

This is not real.

I'm safe.

This is not real.

I grip the edge of the leather recliner and focus on a single green leaf fluttering on an oak in the front yard.

Cool summer breeze. Warm summer sunshine.

I'm safe.

I'm safe.

I'm safe.

My fingers tingle, and my legs wobble, but I can see past the tree now. My lungs expand a little wider, and the rushing in my ears fades as quickly as it arrived.

I'm okay.

I'm okay.

My skin prickles as the last of my panic recedes—it's been two months since the last one, I should've been done with these by now—and a reflected movement in the glass makes me tense up harder.

"Go. Away," I grit out.

Wyatt's at the bottom of the stairs. I didn't hear him coming.

But I hear Wyatt from six months ago.

Fuck, Ellie...shouldn't have done that.

We made a mistake.

You're a mistake.

I squeeze my eyes shut, because he didn't say that.

He didn't say *any* of it beyond *we shouldn't have done that.*

But *why shouldn't we?*

Didn't take much to fill in the blanks.

I was a mistake.

First Patrick—*staying together this long was a mistake. If I was supposed to love you, I wouldn't be in love with someone else*—and then Wyatt. *Fuck, Ellie, that was a mistake.*

"Are you okay?" he asks, and his voice prompts another round of cold chills.

But this isn't the same panicked cold chills still making my thighs and knees quiver, and sending that ache deeper into my left femur.

Nope, that's *regret* cold chills.

"Just a little naked," I reply, because I *am* naked under my robe, and I'm apparently feeling like being an asshole.

I watch his subtle reflection in the window as his head jerks sideways, like he doesn't want to look at me naked.

Who's uncomfortable now?

"Beck didn't mention you'd be here," he tells the wall. "I didn't mean to walk in on you. I thought—I thought one of his old flings had moved in."

I'm fully aware Beck didn't mention me to Wyatt, because he didn't mention Wyatt to me either. I love my brother, but he's obtuse at best and mischievous at worst. "Sounds about right."

There. That was dignified and aloof without being a total asshole.

"Tucker's never been to the Pirate Festival," he adds.

I look past the trees to Shipwreck, nestled amongst more trees in the valley below.

We're 250 miles inland in the Blue Ridge Mountains in southern Virginia, an hour outside the booming metropolis of Copper Valley, overlooking a pirate town called Shipwreck, named thus because of the legend of Thorny Rock.

Thorny Rock, the pirate. Not Thorny Rock, the mountain named after him and which this house is built on. Which is a crucial distinction, since mountains can't smuggle pirate treasure in wagons, nor could they in the eighteenth century when

Thorny Rock founded Shipwreck and supposedly buried all his gold here to hide it from the authorities who were on his trail.

"I'm sure you'll have a lovely time," I tell Wyatt while I tighten my robe ties.

I love the Pirate Festival.

Adore it, even.

But I'm not here for the pirates this week. Or to help dig up the town square—again—in search of Thorny Rock's treasure. Or even to hunt for the peg leg hidden somewhere around town.

Not for myself, I mean. I'm here to be maid of honor while my ex-boyfriend plays best man in my best friend's pirate wedding, since she's marrying his brother.

Apparently while Wyatt gets to dig for treasure and hunt for the peg leg and drink his heart out at The Grog.

Or maybe not the drinking part.

Not when he's here with his son.

That would be a mistake. And Wyatt Morgan doesn't make *mistakes*.

Not twice, anyway.

An uncomfortable silence settles between us. I want to squirm, but I won't give him the satisfaction of knowing he's getting to me.

"You looked like you needed help," he says. "In the bathtub."

I bite my tongue, because my pre-teen years were basically me telling Wyatt *I'll tell you when I need help, now back off*, followed by my early teen years where he grew a foot, discovered weights, got hot, and finally left me to my own devices while he did everything with Lydia.

Pretty, perfect, helpless-without-Wyatt *Lydia*.

Who is none of my business.

Although I'd rather think about Lydia than think about the last time I saw Wyatt.

"Thank you for trying," I say, politely, because it would make my mother proud, and my mother thinks Wyatt hung the fucking moon. And I don't want to argue with him right now. I have to save my energy for tonight. And tomorrow. And the next day. All the way until Friday, when Monica and Jason are getting married in the biggest pirate wedding ever seen in Shipwreck.

"Are you…sticking around for a while?" he asks.

"All week." I study the furniture again, looking for the sparkly cover of my doodle pad, but no luck.

He clears his throat like he's eaten a bad banana pepper.

"But I won't be here much," I add "so…"

"Yeah. Us either."

Wyatt and Ellie, sitting in a tree. A-W-K-W-aaaarrrr-ding!

"Great. I'm actually leaving in…" *Shit.*

My phone.

I don't have a phone.

I can drive. I've been driving again for two months. In a new hybrid car with more airbags than a bagpipe convention and sensors everywhere because other than refusing to drive a gas-guzzling tank, I didn't have it in me to argue when Beck decided it was his job to make sure I had every safety feature known to man, including the freaking *color* of car least likely to be in a car accident.

Except the one feature none of us thought I'd need—internal satellite phone support.

I'll always have my phone, which has a voice assistant, and that's plenty good enough, we all agreed.

I don't drive without a phone.

And I can't call Monica—or Grady, my date for the week—because *I don't have a phone*.

Fuck. *Dammit.*

If I don't show up for dinner and the parade tonight, she'll send someone up here to find me, because that's exactly what I'd do if she was my maid of honor and she didn't show up for a planned event on my itinerary when I knew she was still a little jumpy driving and that she had to come down off a mountain to get there because she desperately needed space from a certain other member of the bridal party and therefore wasn't doing the *easy* thing and spending the week at the Inn.

I didn't tell her I was bringing Grady as my plus-one, just that I was bringing a date, so she won't know she can go to a local for help.

And the only person in the wedding party other than Monica who knows the backroads up the mountain is Patrick.

I flinch at the thought of his name, because while Wyatt was happy to tell me *we shouldn't have done that*, at least he didn't proclaim to love me with all his heart first.

And at least he didn't bring his smart, skinny, beautiful new girlfriend along for the week.

That would be even better.

Look, Ellie, everyone but you is worthy of love. You couldn't even get a fake date without asking four guys first.

I need to get off this mountain.

And get to that dinner.

I turn to head to the kitchen—Beck might have a spare phone in his junk drawer, not because he thinks of things like spare phones, but because he's unpredictable and just when you think he's completely irresponsible, he pulls out a spare cell phone— and for a moment, I forget that my hip doesn't like to move that fast.

My knee buckles, but I catch myself on the end table before I go all the way down.

Wyatt's crossing the room before I can think *boo*, but I hold a hand up. "Foot fell asleep," I lie.

Those gray eyes bore into me, and his full lips go flat. Between the military haircut, the square jaw, the broad shoulders, and that glare, I feel like I should offer to drop and give him twenty.

And no, I don't want to talk about what the combination is doing to my libido. My body doesn't get a vote in this.

It did last time, and that didn't end so well.

And I'm not talking about the accident.

I straighten myself and make my way more slowly to the kitchen.

If he notices the limp, he doesn't comment.

If he notices the *go away* message I'm trying to send him tele-pathically, he also doesn't comment.

Or go away.

"What do you need?" he asks, and I get another shiver, like he's not asking what I'm looking for in the drawer, but what my *soul* needs.

I jerk my head toward the island, where my phone is in a bag of rice.

"Ah. Did you take the SIM card out?"

"Yes, Wyatt, I know enough to know to take the SIM card out."

"Right. Of course you do," he mutters. "You need to call someone?"

I instantly feel like a jerk, because we're not kids fighting over the right way to shoot a free throw or kick a soccer ball anymore, and we're not whoever the hell we were six months ago when he was home for Christmas and Patrick had just dumped me and he'd just gotten a horrific divorce settlement and we were both miserable enough to think we could drown ourselves in meaningless sex between two people who hated each other.

A lot's changed since then.

Mostly me.

"I'm meeting friends in town." I move aside a hand squeezer, fingernail clippers, a set of cards with Beck's picture on them, condoms, and taco sauce packets, among other things, but I'm not finding any spare phones.

Beck changes his number on occasion, and because he's Beck, I'm pretty sure he forgets to cancel his old contracts, but if he has any spare active cell phones, they aren't in this drawer.

I should keep a burner phone up here.

"You lost your keys?" Wyatt says.

"I need a phone."

There's a pause, then a heavy, "Oh."

And now there's also this gigantic guilt giraffe standing in the kitchen, leaning all up in my space.

"Not that it matters, because I don't know anyone's fucking number," I mutter as I realize my *other* problem.

"You want a lift?" he asks. "Tucker wants to see the parade."

I open my mouth to tell him that's not necessary, except...it kinda is.

I can either take his help, or I can scare my friend.

Monica was right on my parents' heels getting to the hospital. She's gone out of her way to have girls' nights—*without* Patrick's new girlfriend—because *just because I'm marrying the idiot's brother doesn't mean I'm giving up my best friend*. And she begged to ride out here to Shipwreck with me because *you are not driving that far alone right now, period*.

She doesn't sugarcoat it.

And I couldn't be more grateful.

And Grady is adorable and kind and well-loved in Shipwreck, and the perfect foil to Patrick and his wonderful new girlfriend, but he's not the kind to panic over me, because he's just a nice guy from town doing me a favor by pretending to be my boyfriend this week.

He's not *actually* interested.

Wyatt's watching me like he always has. Alert. Focused. Aware.

He probably watches everyone like that. I wonder how many other women have had their hearts broken just because of those eyes.

"If it's not too much trouble," I say.

"We're already heading that way."

"Right. Sure. Thanks."

"When do you need to leave?"

"We have reservations at six."

One corner of his mouth hitches. "Crusty Nut?"

I fucking love Shipwreck. And I love that Monica loves it enough to get married here. "Not like The Grog takes reservations or has good seating for the parade."

"We'll be ready at five-thirty."

"Thank you."

It's just a ride. And I'm doing it for Monica.

And I refuse to feel uncomfortable just because he's seen me naked, played wild bucking stallion to my free-range cowgirl, and then decided to return me for a refund.

If he wants to remember that night, that's his problem.

I am officially moving on.

And I am officially not going to let him see that I care anymore.

Because then maybe I can also convince myself.

FOUR

Wyatt

WHILE WE WAIT FOR FIVE-THIRTY, I introduce Tucker to the joy of Pac-Man in Beck's basement haven. Because modeling under-wear as a second career after being in a boy band for years pays well, Beck has money to burn, and he uses it outfitting his houses with enough games to keep a man busy for three lifetimes. In addition to the old-school Pac-Man arcade game console, he has Ms. Pac-Man and Frogger, plus foosball, table tennis, pool, air hockey, and two closets full to bursting with board games. And more.

This whole house is a man cave, but the basement?

The basement is the cherry on top. Half bar with TV viewing area, half game room, it's where we always hang out when we're here on those rare days we're all in the area at the same time without other responsibilities to tackle, and some of my best adult memories have happened in this basement.

Like the Frogger weekend.

And I am *never* risking fucking up that friendship again.

Not for the houses and the games.

But for the guys who are my only family left beyond my son.

"Run away from the ghosts, bud," I tell Tucker, who's sitting on a red leather bar stool so he's tall enough to man the controller. "You can eat them once you get the dot in the corner."

He shrieks with glee as he races the ghosts back and forth on the bottom row, until the blue ghost eats him.

As Pac-Man falls off the screen, Tucker bursts into tears. "I died!" he wails.

"Whoa, hey, it's okay."

"I *died*," he wails harder.

I rub his back, because *fuck*, what else am I supposed to do? It seems like a silly thing to cry over, but then, he's seven. He cried once on spring break because a worm dried out on the sidewalk.

Kid has big feelings and a big heart. There's no way I'm breaking that heart.

The world needs more heart.

"You want to play again?" I ask.

He wipes his eyes, pushing his glasses crooked, and nods. "Uh-huh."

"You want help?"

"Uh-huh."

His hair smells like a fruit pie when I lean over him, and his little body is just so *little*. Even after growing since I saw him last. I kiss his crown and restart the game, covering his small hand with mine. "We're going to run away from the ghosts, okay?"

"Okay."

We die twice more before my phone alarm goes off with my two-minute warning to get upstairs and get shoes on.

Tucker heaves a grown-up sigh. "Really, Dad? The alarms *again*?"

"They keep us on time."

"Sometimes you just have to live life."

And that's his mother coming through. I do my best to keep my expression neutral. "And sometimes, people are counting on us. And other times, we want to get to the pirate parade before we miss it."

He pushes his hair out of his eyes and hops off the stool, dashing for the stairs and clutching his shorts, which are threatening to fall down his slender hips. "Pirate parade! Pirate parade!"

"Tucker, you forgot your..." I trail off, because he's gone, running past the basement bar and up the stairs. So I grab the little scrap of a security blanket he still carries with him and trail after him, also grabbing three dirty glasses from beside a glittery notebook on the high bar counter as I pass, though those aren't our mess. I get to the top of the stairs just a few steps behind Tucker, who's staring again.

And when I look up, I realize why.

"Not. One. Word," Ellie says.

"Daddy, a pirate girl came out of the bathtub," Tucker whispers.

Ellie's eyes go soft as her dimple pops out when she smiles at Tucker. She's in a pirate wench dress, with a fluffy white blouse hanging off her shoulders and covered with one of those leather-looking thingies that ties up from her waist to her chest and gives her good cleavage—a corsage? A coriander? A makes-a-man-speechless?—and a flowing gauzy maroon skirt with black stiletto heels coming up to her knees.

I swallow hard and remind my dick that we're here for my son to go to the Pirate Festival, not for me to lose my head. Again.

Or one of my best friends.

"You may call me Calamity Ellie, captain of the Golden Alba-tross," she says to Tucker, ending on a fancy bow that has her wincing when she stands back up.

I start to ask if those boots are a good idea—she looked like she was hurting earlier, and I know she busted her leg and hip bad in the accident—but then I remember who I'm talking to, and I clamp my mouth shut and move past her to put the glasses in the kitchen.

Especially since she's in full makeup with her hair curled special and hanging down to the tops of her bare shoulders.

She doesn't look like she's meeting friends.

She looks like she's headed for a pirate battle that will be followed with a dance.

Not a care in the world.

Just time to party with the pirates.

"Girls can't be captains," Tucker announces as I step out of the kitchen.

I wince and angle back to put a hand on his shoulder. "Never, *ever* tell a woman she can't be something. Especially Miss —*Captain* Ellie."

"But boys are pirate captains."

Ellie gives me a look that suggests this is *my* fault—of course she does—while she puts her fists to her hips. "Is that so, you scurvy dog? You keep talkin', you'll be swabbing the poop deck!"

Tucker giggles. "Ew, I don't want to swap poop on the deck!"

"Then don't be sayin' there ain't girl pirates, sonny boy."

Ellie winks at him, then sashays past us.

With a limp that puts a rock in my gut.

I've never wanted to protect someone so badly while simultaneously being so irritated with her that I want to tie her to a chair and make her promise she'll quit—quit—fuck.

I don't know what I want her to quit, but I know it's none of my fucking business.

Tucker falls in line behind her and also limps all the way out the door.

Fucking hell.

Does it still hurt? Beck said they weren't sure she'd walk again right after it happened.

But I can't ask.

I don't have the right.

Not with our history. *All* of our history.

"Set the alarm, please, powder monkey," Ellie calls to me as though we're kids again and she's just trying to get my goat.

Like our relationship isn't way more complicated than that.

Like we didn't screw on her parents' basement floor. Like she didn't tear off out of the house right afterward. Like she didn't ignore every last fucking attempt I made to apologize.

"Are you going to the pirate parade with us?" Tucker asks her while I set the alarm and lock up.

"Nay, laddie, I be off to pillage and plunder whilst you all be watching the lesser pirates distract you."

"I'm going to dig for pirate treasure this week."

"Only the luckiest pirates who believe in girl pirate captains will find any gold."

"I know *all* the pirate stories, and none of them are about girl pirates."

"That's because men pirates write all the books."

"Where did you hear all the pirate stories?" I ask Tucker, and not just to distract him from sticking his foot further down his throat, which of course he doesn't realize he's doing, since he's seven. I talk to him most every night before bed, generally read a story on video chat, and I've never read him a pirate story.

"From Mr. Duffy next door. He lets me water his dog and he tells me about when he was fighting all the pirates before the war."

"Which war?"

"The Civil War."

I make a mental note to ask my ex-wife if she's aware of what Tucker's doing when he's playing outside. She'll probably tell me Mr. Duffy's a harmless old man, but Tucker can't always tell the difference between reality and a good story, and I don't want him getting made fun of at school for talking about his neighbor the vampire pirate hunter.

I fucking *hate* not being close enough to go see his teachers and just be there for those minutes after school when he talks about his day.

One more year.

Just one more year.

"Keys?" Ellie says to me.

"I locked the door."

She points to my SUV. "So I can drive."

"No."

"That wasn't a question."

"This is *my car*."

"I have control issues."

She's got that stubborn look Beck gets when he's determined that we're going to play poker until he wins. And she's not overtly setting any guilt trips, but she doesn't have to.

She doesn't fucking have to.

I approach and dangle my keys between us. "I'm backseat driving."

She smirks. "Of course you are."

But she still takes the keys.

I hold the ring steady until she makes eye contact again. "That's my kid you're driving," I add softly.

She holds my gaze without flinching. "Noted. Now, if you don't want me stealing this thing, you better get in."

Tucker's already in the backseat strapping into his booster seat, so I settle into the passenger seat.

Feels weird to be on this side of the car.

But I think I owe her.

She might not realize it yet, but she owes me too.

And since we're here together, she's going to pay up.

FIVE

Ellie

SHIPWRECK SMELLS LIKE FRIED OYSTERS, cannon fire, and dirt. People in pirate costumes stroll along Blackbeard Avenue while locals leap out from behind barrels and out of the local shops to challenge tourists to swordfights.

It's glorious.

I tell Wyatt and Tucker to go on about their business, that I'll get a ride back with a friend, but because Wyatt is Wyatt, he insists on walking with me from the parking fields at the end of the main drag toward Crusty Nut, which has the best fried pickles and banana pudding in all of Virginia, and yes, I *have* sampled every banana pudding in Copper Valley, and a fair number up in the DC metro area too, so I *can* say with absolute certainty that Crusty Nut's banana pudding cannot be beat.

Also, if you don't like banana pudding, I'm happy to eat yours. You can have my Twizzlers.

"Tucker, have you ever seen the inside of a pirate ship?" I ask as we pass Scuttle Putt, the miniature golf course at the edge of the park. The entrance to the payment shack is shaped like the bow of a ship, complete with a mermaid figurehead above the door.

Tucker slows.

Wyatt scoops him up and puts him on his shoulders like he's light as a feather. "We'll check it out later."

"Why are you doing this?" I murmur. "I don't need a fu—freaking escort. I'm *fine*."

"Your brother would kick my *ahem* if I didn't get you back safe and sound to his house tonight, and we both know it."

"I know everyone in town, and I'll get a ride. Go away."

"Not until I see who's driving you home."

I pause outside Crow's Nest, the local bakery, as I spot the owner just inside the open door, wiping down tables in a pirate costume, complete with eye patch.

Just as he's supposed to be. "Hey, Grady. You ready?"

I smile, and he smiles back, and for the first time since Wyatt walked in on me in the bathtub, I know tonight's going to be okay.

"You bet, hot stuff. Give me two seconds to toss this rag."

Wyatt looks at me.

Then at Grady, who's six solid feet of dependable, adorable muscle and dimples, topped with a thick mop of dark hair that even his hairnet can't fully contain.

"What the f—fudge is going on here?" he growls.

"Just picking up my date. Who will also drive me home."

"Your *date*."

"Mm-hmm. Like I said, go about your business."

Cooper, Grady's brother, strolls out of the bakery and rubs my hair. Not because he's older than me, but because he's taller than me. "Still heartbroken you didn't pick me, Calamity Ellie."

"You're unreliable," I reply, earning a laugh.

"Dad. *Dad*," Tucker whispers reverently while Wyatt continues to glare. "*Daaaad*."

"I'm still handsomer," Cooper points out.

I pretend to study him, then shake my head. "Nah."

He puts a hand to his heart like he's wounded. "Aah, Ellie. What's a guy gotta do to get your affections?"

"You have to pick up your phone when she calls, idiot," Grady tells his brother as he steps outside, sans the hairnet under his pirate hat. He offers me an arm. "Shall we, Calamity Ellie?"

"Who the hell are you?" Wyatt snarls.

"He's—" I start, but I'm suddenly squished in a bride-scented hug with a fake parrot smashed into my face.

"Ellie! There you are. Why aren't you answering your phone?" Monica demands. She's dressed to the hilt as a pirate captain, with her honey blond hair tied back in a low ponytail under her pirate hat.

"It's recovering from a swim," I tell her.

"Daddy and Miss Ellie took a bubble bath together!" Tucker announces as I pull back.

Monica's hazel eyes dart from me to Wyatt to Tucker up on Wyatt's shoulders, going round as a pirate steering wheel by the time they're back on me.

Grady drops his arm and takes a step back, brows raised, a slow smile spreading like he's coming to a conclusion.

Shit.

Shit on a cannonball. This is *not* how today is supposed to go.

Behind Monica, Patrick, tall, blond, and usually affectedly bored, narrows his eyes like I'm still his business. "A bubble bath? Together?"

"They were all covered in bubbles," Tucker says with a giggle.

I laugh too, way too high. "And isn't it dinner time?" I interrupt, because I am *not* going to dinner solo with my ex-boyfriend and his perfect girlfriend and once again, Wyatt Morgan is fucking up my life. He's going to ruin my carefully crafted date routine with Grady for the week. "We should get down to Crusty Nut before the parade starts."

The crowd's getting thicker, so I'm not wrong.

But Monica, Jason—her fiancé, who's dressed like a first mate but usually looks like a surfer—Patrick, and his girlfriend, Sloane, don't move.

"You're dating again?" Patrick asks, again like it's his business.

"Dude, I didn't realize," Grady says, backing away while Cooper shakes with silent laughter at his brother's expense.

"Wyatt and I are *friends*," I say lightly in a tone that leaves my answer open for interpretation.

Wyatt lifts a brow at me while holding onto Tucker's legs, because whatever we are, we've never really been *friends*. More like people with opposing personalities who sometimes cross paths in social circles since my brother has always thought he could do no wrong.

But if he's screwing up my fake date for the week, he's going to be something other than my *friend*.

"Why doesn't your *friend* join us for dinner?" Patrick says tightly, and *that's right, you dumping asshole, I have men fighting over me*.

Sloane angles closer to him. "They're not in costume," she points out.

Like all of us, she too is dressed like a pirate. Her costume has red-and-black striped pants loose around her thighs but fitted to her calves, a white blouse, and a leather strap over her shoulder holding her scabbard and fake sword. A matching bandana covers her hair, and she's sporting skull and crossbones earrings.

Patrick's costume is nearly identical, except he's missing the earrings.

And I can't say a thing, because I would've dressed us in matching pirate costumes too.

"Grady was coming with me for dinner," I say, "because Wyatt and Tucker have never seen the pirate parade, and Pop's less likely to harass Grady if he's with us. Wyatt, really, that's an amazing spot to watch the parade. Tucker will love it. And wait until you see Pop. Pop Rock? Grady and Cooper's grandpa? He dresses up like Blackbeard every year. It's glorious."

I point desperately to a minute space between a lamp post and a family of six right at the curb.

"Wyatt...Wyatt Morgan?" Monica asks.

And I'm done. Totally, completely screwed. My master plan for a fake boyfriend this week is unraveling before my eyes.

So I do the only thing I can to save my pride in the face of disaster.

I link my arm through Wyatt's. "It's new," I whisper, telling my best friend of ten years a bald-faced lie that will undoubtedly kick me in the lady nuts very, very soon. Like as soon as Wyatt opens his mouth and bucks away from me. "And I didn't want to take away from his time with Tucker this week."

There's a muscle working in Wyatt's jaw, but his gray eyes aren't glaring.

Nope, they're shifting into neutral. He disentangles himself from my arm, but then wraps his tightly about my shoulders, which is a little awkward with Tucker up on his shoulders, but he manages anyway. Because he's Wyatt.

Of *course* he can hold a kid *and* me.

"I don't share," he says with a pointed look at Grady.

Cooper has a coughing fit.

"*Dad*," Tucker howls, kicking Wyatt in the pec. "That's *Cooper Rock*."

"I'm free tonight, Ellie," Cooper says. He winks at Wyatt.

"And you're staying free," Wyatt replies pleasantly.

Too pleasantly.

Like he's bantering with Beck and the guys.

"Wyatt Morgan?" Monica repeats again.

"I know that name," Patrick says with a frown.

I shrug and put on what I hope is an embarrassed smile, rather than the mortified dread I'm feeling at the farce I'm going to have to pull off *all fucking week* if I don't want to be the fifth wheel for my best friend's wedding to my ex-boyfriend's brother. "You know what they say about that line between love and hate."

Monica's hazel eyes are so wide under her feathered pirate wench hat that she's in danger of losing an eyeball. "Well, yeah, I mean, I always suspected as much, but…*oh my god*, Ellie! I'm so fuc—freaking happy for you!"

She tackles me in a hug, babbling about needing all the details while I reel a little, because what the hell does *I always suspected as much* mean?

"Monica, seriously, this is *your* week. Wyatt and I are just… we're taking it slow. He doesn't *really* care if Grady comes to dinner with us."

Wyatt's grip—yep, he's still holding on, despite Monica trying to strangle me with a hug too—tightens so hard that if my shoulders were walnuts, they'd be walnut butter. "Yes, I do."

"DAD, THAT'S COOPER ROCK!" Tucker hollers.

Cooper, who no longer has any shot of anonymity, steps out from behind his brother to offer Tucker a fist bump. "Give it up, little buddy. You like the Fireballs?"

Tucker nods solemnly while he looks at his fist. "Dad says loyalty's important, even in the face of great loss."

Cooper pounds his heart twice with his fist. "Dang straight. Your dad's a smart guy."

"You'll get 'em this year," Tucker declares.

Cooper winces. Grady winces. Half the street winces.

Since Chicago won the World Series a few years ago, Copper Valley's pro baseball team has taken over as the sport's most lovable losers.

And they're embracing the title with gusto this year.

"They will, won't they, Tucker?" I say.

"They really will." He beams at me like we're going to be best friends, and I think he could be right.

Monica's frowning. "I don't know if Crusty Nut can fit two more people at our table."

"It's okay," I tell her quickly. "Tucker will love the parade *so* much more from right here. He can't catch as much booty if he's up on the balcony with us. Wyatt's okay with this, aren't you, honey?"

I lift my eyes to his, and that's a mistake.

Because he's promising me a lot of retribution in that colorful gray gaze. And if you think gray can't be colorful, you've never pissed off a gray-eyed man.

"Looks like I have to be," he replies.

"But you have to join us for lunch tomorrow," Monica announces. She squeezes my hand. "Oh my god, Ellie, I always thought this might happen." She throws herself around Wyatt too, and the parrot wobbling on her shoulder, stitched to her pirate captain costume, pecks Tucker's bare calf. "You better be good to her, or I'll slice your nuts off with my pirate sword and tie a cannonball to your ankles and shoot you over the mountains."

Tucker gasps.

"She's teasing," Wyatt tells him quickly.

Monica smiles.

It's an ugly smile.

I like it.

Wyatt smiles back.

It's a tight smile.

My life is going to be hell as soon as I get back to Beck's place tonight.

"Can you drive me home?" I ask Monica. "Tucker has an early bedtime."

"Of course!" she squeals.

Patrick's still glaring.

And since Patrick's glaring, Sloane the wonder nurse is also glaring.

Only Jason, Monica's laid-back fiancé who's been watching all of this with an amused smile, is still blissfully unaware of all the weirdness.

It's remarkable that Patrick and Jason share genes, because that's the only thing they have in common.

"You'll drive safely," Wyatt informs Monica.

She rolls her eyes at him. "First one to the hospital. I got it."

He finally releases his grip on me.

"Go on, get that spot," I tell him. "Tucker, you're going to love the parade."

"Can we all have a bubble bath tonight?" he asks.

"No," Wyatt and I answer together.

The adults lining the parade route all chuckle with Grady, Cooper, Monica, and Jason. "You are adorable," Monica informs Tucker. "We're going to be good friends this week."

She's not going to see them at all this week if I have any say in it.

Far better to have a boyfriend who's an amazing single dad from afar than to have to put on a show for my friend and my ex-boyfriend anyway.

Maybe this will work out after all.

"Enjoy the parade," I tell Wyatt. "I'll see you back at the house."

His lips twitch, because Wyatt and I don't do *see you later*.

We never have.

As kids, we'd part on me shouting *shut up and let me do it my way* to his *fine, do it your way and lose, you crazy buttwipe.* As adults, there's less shouting, but generally more eye-rolling.

Until that last time.

Over Christmas.

He bends down and kisses my cheek. "I'll miss you, schmoopsy-poo." Quieter, he adds, "And we're discussing this later."

"I'll miss you too," I say breathlessly.

Monica loops her arm around mine and tugs gently, prodding me into falling into step beside her.

Well, limp.

These shoes were a terrible idea.

I give Grady a quick, "Sorry about that," over my shoulder, but he just grins and waves me off.

"Good to see you happy, Ellie."

I don't look at Wyatt.

I can't.

"Why didn't you ever tell me he was hot?" Monica asks, because she came into my life after Wyatt was already gone in the military, and I realize with a start that she's never actually met him.

"Most of my life, I didn't look at him that way," I answer honestly.

"I'm gonna need this bubble bath story."

"I'm sure it's nothing you've never done yourself," I reply.

"Your leg hurts, doesn't it?"

"What's pain when I look like a million Spanish galleons?"

She rolls her eyes, then glances back.

I look back too, and spot Wyatt buying a foam sword for Tucker from a passing street vendor.

Except he's not buying just one.

He's buying two.

He swings Tucker down, squats and holds his sword in the ready position, and then staggers in mock pain as Tucker gets him in the gut.

"Right," Monica murmurs, fanning herself. "Not hot at all."

That's right.

He's not hot at all.

I just have to pretend he is.

It's only four days. And barely a few little lies.

It'll all be just fine.

SIX

Wyatt

I DON'T like leaving Ellie in Shipwreck, but she's a grown-up, she's with friends, and one of the guys from the bakery—Cooper? Fuck, I haven't kept up with the Fireballs this year—came out to chat for a while during the parade, and while I won't admit it to Ellie, he passed my gut test.

Seems like a decent guy.

So does his brother, Grady, who apologized again for the mix-up and told me I was a lucky guy.

So she has good people looking out for her in a safe small town, and she'll be okay.

But after I read six bedtime stories with Tucker, promise we'll go miniature golfing and try to dig up pirate treasure and look for the hidden peg leg that's supposed to come with a treasure of its own tomorrow, and hug him tight because it's *so* damn good to be able to hug him—video chat and phone calls aren't the same, and now that he's starting soccer and baseball, there's less time to talk—I head to the living room to wait for Ellie to get back.

It's possible she won't *come* back tonight.

Cooper wasn't shy with information, and while Tucker raked

in candy, pirate rings, fake gemstones, and more from the floats passing by, I found out Ellie's in town for her best friend's wedding. Most of the wedding party is staying at the Shipwreck Inn. Her ex-boyfriend—I thought the Blond Caveman looked familiar—is the best man and brought the woman he dumped her for just before her accident. Ellie's been in town a lot the last six months—especially while she was recovering at first—and Cooper's glad Beck sent someone to keep an eye on her while she's feeling so lost.

That last part is what has me dialing my buddy, even though I think he's somewhere in Europe on a photo shoot and it's probably two in the morning at the earliest wherever he is.

Hell, I don't even know if his cell number works in Europe.

But, because he's Beck, he answers on the second ring.

"Wyatt, my man, what's up? How's the house?" Beck says in my ear.

I glance at the mess in the kitchen, and I shove up to tackle it, because it's annoying me. "Occupied."

Beck laughs. "If you're there, it must be."

"Ellie's here."

There's silence, and for half a second, I think he's going to pull the *Connection's breaking up* card, but then he simply says, "Huh."

Not like he's surprised.

Not like he's not either.

I stack up plates, cups, mugs—someone likes tea, it seems—silverware and dirty napkins from the dining room and carry them into the kitchen.

I don't have room to call Beck on any bullshit—it's my fault his sister was in a car accident that put her in the hospital for a month and still has her limping—but if he wants something from me, he damn well needs to come out and ask before I fuck this up.

Again.

"Ryder…"

"You remember that year we played Trivial Pursuit over Christmas break and you and Ellie ended up having a ranch dressing fight in the snow?"

"She called me a cheater."

"Bro, you did cheat."

"I did not."

"You memorized the cards."

"There was nothing else to read."

"Whatever. The point is, think of all the good memories. How about that time she went apeshit because you were using her art projects for target practice?"

"*You* brought them out and didn't mention they were—"

"Good times, good times." He sighs happily. "Man, I wish I could be there with you guys. Wonder if you'd wrestle me over Frogger again like that time—"

"What the fuck are you smoking?"

"Fresh air, man. The best fresh night air Spain has to offer. You ever been to Spain? It's fucking gorgeous."

Fucker's avoiding my questions.

He *knew* Ellie would be here. And he knows we can't stand each other. I stifle a growl of frustration while I plug the sink, squirt soap in, and flip on the faucet.

"I found her in the bathtub," I grit out. I can tell him I found her in the bathroom, but I *will not* confess to my best friend that we've gone a lot farther than that.

Being friends with Beck Ryder saved my life, and it doesn't matter if we go a few months without talking, that will never change.

Nor will I *ever* do anything to potentially fuck it up again.

I keep waiting for Ellie to tell him, for him to turn on me, but apparently she either doesn't remember or doesn't want him to know.

So I'm not going to tell him either.

"You found her in the bathtub? Doing Jell-O shots or something?"

Beck might play the egotistical, idiot underwear model, but I've known him for too many years for me to fall for this bullshit. "Naked."

"Ah. Yeah, that makes more sense. Were you naked too?"

"Christ on a butter knife, you jackass. Who asks that?"

"Wyatt. You're my bro. You think we'd be friends if I didn't think you were good enough for my sister? Nah, man. I've seen how you two look at each other. Far be it from me to interfere."

I'm momentarily speechless, because I didn't think that was how the bro code worked. And Beck and a few other guys we grew up with made a name for themselves as the band Bro Code for a lot of years.

So don't tell me the bro code isn't important to him.

It's *everything*.

He's gotta be fucking with me, so I go with the easy response. "She looks at me like she'd like to slice out my kidneys and roast them over a campfire."

"Young love, man. Young love is beautiful."

"Ryder."

"Dude. It ever occur to you that maybe it would mean a lot to me if one of my best buddies could finally just suck it up and get along with my sister? Is that too much to ask?"

I briefly consider Levi or Davis or one of the Rivers brothers asking Ellie on a date, and I decide it doesn't matter that they, too, are like brothers to me, I'd smash all their faces in.

"What the fuck's actually going on?" I ask.

I wash six glasses while I wait for him to answer, and when he finally does, I wish I hadn't asked.

"You know that accident Ellie was in?"

The pit of my stomach drops just like it did when I got his text the day after I fucked up. "We all know about Ellie's accident, man."

"She's been...reserved since then."

"She wasn't fucking reserved when she punched me for trying to save her from drowning and then dunked me in the tub," I say dryly.

"Really? That's great!"

I swipe a hand over my face, because I'm getting annoyed. Beck's always lived in his own world, but this is extreme, even for him. "She dropped her phone in the tub, so it might be a while before she calls to bitch you out."

"Even better," he says cheerfully.

"Push comes to shove, she tells me to leave, you know I'm gone."

"Whoa, whoa, hold up." Beck's suddenly serious as banana pudding, which is pretty fucking serious in these parts. "Okay, okay. Yes, I knew Ellie was going to be there. That's why I kept talking up the pirate festival for Tucker. She…needs you."

"Your sister. Eleanor *I can do it myself* Ryder. She needs me."

"Wyatt. She doesn't *know* it, but yeah, she needs you. She's just—she hasn't been herself since the accident. And that prick Patrick dumping her right at the holidays for his neighbor—she's always had this life plan, you know? Finish school, take over for Mom and Dad, get married, have three kids, live happily ever after. But it's all…I mean, work's good. It's about all she does anymore. I told you she qualified to run the New York City Marathon this year, didn't I? Qualified back before the accident. Now she can't do it. She's just…it's like she's giving up. She puts on the show, but she doesn't talk about her plans anymore like she used to."

I grunt, because yeah, Ellie was *always* making plans. *When I'm in high school, I'm going to be on the soccer team. When I'm in college, I'm going to make the Dean's list. When I go to work for Mom and Dad, I'm going to convince City Hall to hire us to make the building green. When I get married, I'm going to have two-point-four kids and a dog and a parakeet named Sue.*

"You know what I'm talking about," Beck says. "And the thing is…you irritate the shit out of her. So maybe…I don't know. Just give her something *normal*. Annoy her until she starts planning on annoying you back. And I know she's there at that wedding with her dickweed ex too. Drop-kick him for me a couple times, would you?"

I drop a clean plate into the drying rack before it registers that Ellie hasn't been cleaning her own dishes.

Ellie doesn't leave messes. She's too type A for that.

Something *is* wrong. "You know there's something really fucked up about asking me to irritate your sister."

"I wouldn't trust another soul for this job. Because I know you won't hurt her. Irritate the fuck out of her, yeah. But hurt her? Not you, man."

Fucking *damn* it.

I already did that, didn't I?

"Are you serious?"

"Everyone's treating her with kid gloves. She needs to know she can still do stuff."

"She's down in town in high heel pirate boots. I think she knows she can still do stuff."

"Yeah, and I'm just a dumbass egomaniac who models underwear."

Right. The Ryders know how to put on a face for the world. Doesn't mean that's the real story.

"I'm not going to try to pick fights with your sister to make her feel better." Especially not when she's just told the bride that *I'm her fucking boyfriend.*

Which I'm still in denial about, because I'm not spending this week confusing my kid.

But I don't like how her ex was looking at her.

I don't want to let him think she's easy pickings right now either.

Beck laughs. "Like you have to try to irritate her. Just be you. It'll happen."

"Why don't *you* try to annoy her?"

"Can't. She's my baby sister, and she's hurt. My instinct is to protect and save."

"You just asked *me* to annoy her."

"That's different. Plus, it was Levi's idea. Fuck, I thought you two loved each other. I forgot all those times she threw dog poop at you when we were playing volleyball and you tried to help her serve better."

I can't believe I'm smiling over *that* memory, but here we are. "I was honestly surprised the day I heard she actually graduated college without getting arrested."

"Mom says she never found where she fit in. Toss in teenage hormones and having us for role models, and she was basically doomed. But I think Levi's right. She always hated you the most."

"Appreciate that."

"She can't go too hard on you. Not with Tucker around. She loves kids."

And I can't go too hard on her.

Not with Tucker around.

Kid needs a good role model, not a fucked-up one. Especially since I know his mother's dating again.

But the only thing I learned about being a good role model, I learned from my buddies' fathers. Not my own.

"She's gonna be okay, Beck," I tell him. "She's too stubborn not to be."

"Thanks, man. I owe you one."

"No, you don't."

"Quit being a pain in the ass. And don't beat my high score on Frogger or I'll ship you a box of dicks at work."

"You coming home anytime this summer?"

"Sometime."

"Swing by Georgia when you do. I need you to show Tucker that all these pillows and cardboard cutouts of you are airbrushed so he doesn't get body image issues. And bring your baby book. The one with the picture of you swimming in cake with your baby belly hanging over your diaper."

He laughs. "You got it."

I hang up and finish the dishes, clean out the fireplace, and take out the trash before settling in to listen to an audiobook in the darkened living room.

Because if Ellie's coming home tonight, we're going to talk.

About everything.

SEVEN

Ellie

IN ADDITION to my brain reeling from trying to keep my story about Wyatt straight all night, my thigh and hip are full-on throbbing by the time Monica pulls to a stop beside Wyatt's SUV in Beck's driveway. A single lamp shines in the front window and the porch light glows bright in the dark, starless night. Once she has the car in park, she turns to look at me. "Sorry I didn't get you home in time to take advantage of Wyatt."

"Parenting is exhausting. We'll have plenty of time later. And Wyatt knows I'm here for *you* this week. Like I know he's here for Tucker to see the Pirate Festival. It's just a bonus that we get any time at all."

Gag me. But she'll freak more if she knows I'm faking this, and I do *not* want to distract her from the joy of her pirate wedding week.

She leans over to hug me tight. "Thank you so much for being here this week."

"Are you kidding? I wouldn't miss this for the world."

"Am I a horrible person if I say I could really like Sloane if she wasn't dating Patrick?" she whispers.

"Patrick's going to be your *brother-in-law*. So probably."

"I meant the being disloyal to you part."

"Oh, stop. I have Wyatt. Patrick has Sloane. The world has moved on. Besides, I think I could like her too. Did you hear her story about the patient who kept trying to trade her chocolate bars for tequila? That was really funny."

"But I'm still on Team Ellie."

"We're not on *teams*."

"But I'm totally on Team Wyatt. I swear, Ellie, if he turns into a douche too after all this build-up—"

"What build-up?"

"You don't spend years claiming to hate a man, then screw his brains out, then nearly get yourself killed in an accident and refuse to even admit you screwed his brains out for *months* afterward, and not have secret feelings for him. You just don't."

I gape at her.

"This isn't about the accident, is it?" she asks, her brow furrowing in the dim light. "Because if he's doing this because he feels guilty, and not because he's always been unable to handle knowing that you're his soul mate, then I might have to slice his balls off. And I don't want to do that. Not when I think of the trauma to his kid."

"You are such a nut."

"And you love me for it."

I really do. She's like a female version of Beck. Fun, intentionally obtuse, and sometimes annoying, but always with good intentions, and always there to have your back.

I could do without the inference that Wyatt and I are soul mates though, because while it's fantastic for a cover story, it's horrible for my indigestion. "I hope I can be as good a friend as you someday," I tell her.

"Hush your mouth. Who's limping around on pirate boots to appease the bride?"

"I'm not limping."

"You will be when I kick you out of this car so I can go back to town and break into Jason's room for crazy parrot sex."

"*Crazy parrot sex*?"

"Huh. I was going for monkey sex with a pirate theme. That didn't quite work, did it?"

I give her one last hug before I swing the door open. "I love you, you goober. Go seduce your fiancé until you can't walk tomorrow."

"Well, if I must." She winks. "Help you to the door?"

"*No.* I've got this. You go."

"And you go have crazy parrot sex too. Understand me? And call me if you need a ride tomorrow. I mean, if Wyatt's willing to let you out of his sight again."

I lift the bag of two burner phones I grabbed to keep here, because *no* guest should ever be without access to a phone. "I should be fine, and my phone will be all dried out by tomorrow night. But thank you."

After I assure her that yes, I also now have her phone number, Jason's phone number, and Grady's phone number written on a piece of paper to give to Wyatt and program into both of the burner phones I picked up at Peg Legs and Planks—yes, the hardware store here sells burner phones—I climb out of her car.

I make it to the front door without limping despite the pain shooting from my knee to my tailbone, but I refuse to let Monica see me hurting. It's her wedding week, and she doesn't need to worry over me.

I wave as I push open the door. She reverses in the darkness to head back down the mountain to town, and as soon as I'm inside, I crumple to a heap against the wall beside the door and let out a soft groan.

The bedroom is a long fucking way away. Past at least seven massive floor tiles in the foyer, then down a hallway the length of six football fields, through the door, and a walk from here to China to get to the bed.

Or so it feels.

Five minutes.

I just need five minutes to sit here, kneading my twisted thigh muscle and resting my achy hip joint, and then I'll be fine.

"Need help?"

I shriek in surprise at the voice coming out of the semi-darkness, and I realize I'm not alone.

Wyatt's up.

Dammit.

"Just wondering the last time Beck's maids dusted the floor-boards. Plus, you get a totally different angle on that artwork." I point to a row of prints on the wall outside the kitchen.

"The three-piece selfie of Beck's nostril?"

"Most people think it's a cave."

"Most people don't know Beck very well."

He's barefoot, in cargo shorts and a polo with a military-looking logo on his breast pocket, and when he tucks his thumbs in his belt loops and leans against the wall, my ovaries do a back-flip, because yes, Wyatt Morgan *is* quite the handsome man.

And possibly I shouldn't have had that glass of wine three hours ago. Clearly it's still affecting my judgment.

"Overdid it?" he asks.

My eyes narrow and I start to scowl, and then the oddest thing happens.

Instead of narrowing his eyes right back at me, his lips twitch like he's holding in a smile, he lifts his eyes to the ceiling, mutters, "Dammit, Beck," and suddenly I'm more curious than I am irritated.

Until he squats down and picks me up, that is.

I yelp and try to twist, but I jolt my leg wrong and I end up gasping for breath and gripping him around the neck instead. "What are you doing?" I grit out.

"Annoying you," he says as he straightens and moves toward the hall.

He hasn't shaved. I could try to count his short whiskers if I wanted to. He's always clean-shaven. Maybe he's being a pirate this week too.

"You are *not* welcome in my bedroom."

"That's seventy miles away or so, isn't it? Which part of Copper Valley is your house in again?"

"Quit being a smart-ass."

"There's no shame in taking help when you need it."

"I don't need help."

I am such a liar. Every step he takes closer to the bedroom is like a weight being lifted off my shoulders. *One less step I have to take…two less…three…*

"It's your boyfriend's duty to carry you to the bedroom."

"Don't even—" I start.

His lips twitch again.

Right there. Right in front of my face. His lips are twitching.

Like I *amuse* him.

I don't amuse anyone. Annoy them, yes. It was one of the reasons Patrick broke up with me. *Ellie, you're just…so perfectionist, it's annoying.* I'm well aware that my project managers back home at work are relieved as hell that I'm on vacation, but I also know that having high standards is the only way I'm going to continue my parents' legacy and grow their business when they retire in a few years.

Which is in a few years.

Not right here.

Tonight.

With Wyatt not even breaking a sweat or straining while he carries me into the master bedroom, despite the weight I've gained since the accident.

"Thank you," I grumble when he sets me gently on the bed.

"You're not really welcome."

I gasp in surprise.

He purses his lips together and turns, but not before I see his gray eyes twinkling.

Twinkling.

Like he's *enjoying* being a shit.

"I should ask you to fetch my pajamas, but I sleep naked, so there's no point," I announce.

"You want a cowbell so you can call me to hang up your dress when you've flung it across the room?"

There's no heat in his words. It's like we're playing a game not to see who can be more insulting, but who can be more outrageous.

Because there's no way in hell *anyone* would give me a cowbell.

There's also no way in hell he's *flirting* with me, which is the other possibility reeling through my mind.

"I prefer a foghorn." I bend to tug my boot off, and another splinter of pain makes me suck in a breath.

I really, really overdid it tonight.

Without looking at my face, Wyatt bends over my feet and tugs my boots off, first my right foot, then ever-so-carefully my left foot.

I duck my head, because there's a sudden burn in my eyes that's drifting into my sinuses as well. "Please don't be nice to me," I whisper. "Not when we're alone. Though you owe me pretending to be my boyfriend this week, because that was a shitty thing to do to Grady."

"I just wanted to confirm your feet stink. And they do."

I shove him without thinking, because that's what we do. "They do not."

"I called you."

And now I want to hit him for real, because the shift in his tone means he did just say exactly what I thought he just said, about exactly what I've been afraid he'll want to talk about, and we are *not* talking about this. "My phone got busted in the accident. It's apparently a recurring problem."

"Beck had you a new phone with your same number sitting by your bed the minute you were conscious."

"So?"

"So, I tried calling you for *weeks*."

I swallow hard, because he's not taking my easy excuses. And the truth isn't nice. "I didn't want to talk to you."

"You usually don't. But—"

"No buts. Thank you. I can get my dress."

"I didn't mean to hurt you."

"All water under the bridge. You were right. It was a mistake. Didn't happen. Moving on. Okay?"

He takes my chin in his fingers and lifts my face until I can't help but look at him while he studies me with those intense gray eyes.

His lashes are stupidly thick. They're not long, but they're thick. And his nose is slightly off-center, but not in a weird way. Just in a rugged way.

And his lips—

I'm breathing too loud. And he's watching me too closely.

Like he can see way down deep to the fourteen-year-old girl inside who turned around one day and realized that one of my older brother's best friends was cute. And a little awkward, and still annoying with the way he *always* seemed to know *everything*, but also reliable and familiar but...new.

And dating Lydia Baker, who was smart and pretty and on the cheerleading squad. Not the head cheerleader, but still a cheerleader.

He was seventeen to my fourteen, which was basically illegal, and because I've always been *that* girl who knew *everything*, yes, I knew he was illegal, and I knew why I got all warm in my belly when he looked at me, and I was also pissed that I couldn't control my body's reaction to him.

But I don't feel like I know anything tonight.

I don't know who I am.

I don't know why I'm here.

I don't know what I want.

Not past the next five minutes, anyway.

It's not the first time I've felt this way.

And the last time ended with me broken.

"Was it my fault?" he asks.

"You weren't driving the car, Wyatt."

"But it was my fault you were."

It wasn't. He didn't force me into the car. He didn't choose my route. He didn't *make* me do anything.

He even tried to stop me.

"It takes two. Quit being the martyr."

"Nobody trusted Beck to give us the truth about how you were doing. And you wouldn't answer your phone. I was scared shitless."

"I'm *fine*. Same old annoying Ellie."

And there he goes again, seeing right through me. "Yeah. Same old annoying Ellie."

Fuck. I whimper out a laugh, because it's so damn *normal* to have Wyatt calling me annoying that I'm in danger of crying. "Shut up."

"Annoying, know-it-all Ellie," he adds.

I reach out to shove his shoulder, but there's no speed or force behind my hand, and I end up resting it on his bicep instead. "Mansplaining Wyatt," I whisper.

His eyes are boring into mine the same way they did that night while he plants his hands on either side of my legs. "Planner Ellie."

"Stick up your butt Wyatt."

"Refuses to take help Ellie."

"Refuses to admit anyone else can know how to do anything Wyatt."

Our faces are drifting closer. This is a bad idea. We've been here before, and it ended in disaster. *Worse* than disaster. I need to shove him away for real.

Or…we need to practice so that on the rare occasions this week when we *have* to be seen together in public for whatever reason—Shipwreck isn't *that* big—we can fake affection.

"Jumps to conclusions Ellie." His breath tickles my nose.

"Obnoxious—" I start, but I stop when our lips touch.

A shudder races through me, but it's not a bad shudder. It's not a good shudder either. It's my body craving human affection while my mind recoils in fear, because the last time I was here, with Wyatt, his perfect lips rubbing mine, his hot breath lighting up my veins, it literally changed the entire course of my life.

Maybe this is what I need to do.

Maybe kissing him will end this weird limbo I've been in. It'll make the pain in my leg go away. I'll find my balance at work again. The stars will realign, the man of my dreams will walk in the front door, I'll start running again, and I'll be living the life I always wanted to have.

I won't *care* that Patrick's life went on perfectly with his nurse girlfriend. I won't *care* that my injuries might be more than skin and bone deep. I won't care that I have to pick a new future for myself.

My free hand loops around his neck and drifts up to rub the prickles of his short hair. He suckles my lower lip and leans me back to the pillow, deepening the kiss as we go.

This isn't the kiss we had at Christmas.

No, this is a *who are you?* kiss. It's an *I've been worried sick over you* kiss. A *let's do this right* kiss.

I've hated this man most of my life, from the day his grandmother knocked on our door and asked Beck if he could come out and play with the short, wide-eyed, floppy brown-haired boy with the stained T-shirt, through my pre-teen years when he grew into an obnoxious know-it-all, into my teen years when he didn't even acknowledge I existed anymore.

I shouldn't like kissing him.

Last time he kissed me, he told me it was a mistake.

And it was. It was the biggest mistake of my life.

But now I'm stroking my tongue against his and my breasts are aching for his touch and my clit is pulsing with a desperate need for attention.

I haven't had sex in six months.

Not since Wyatt.

Not since the accident.

I part my legs, and pain erupts in my left thigh. I break the kiss with a gasp, Wyatt and I make eye contact, and he leaps off the bed. A brief flash of terror skitters over his face before he rubs his hands into his eyes and takes one more step toward the door. "Do you have pain meds somewhere?"

"That bad, was it?" I deadpan while I rub my thigh.

He watches my hands and doesn't even spare me a dirty look. "For your leg."

"I'm *fine*."

He mutters a curse and stalks into the bathroom. I hear him riffling through my crap, and I don't bother telling him to stay out of my stuff since he won't listen anyway, and a pain pill sounds like heaven.

Not quite as much heaven as him kissing me, which is a paradox I don't want to deal with right now, but I take some comfort in knowing he'll see my vibrator if he looks hard enough, and let him think about *that* all night long.

He returns, slaps a prescription bottle on the nightstand, and marches out of the room.

My body sags, and I realize I must look crazy in my pirate wench costume. My mascara's probably running, and who knows what's happened to my lipstick.

I'm unscrewing the bottle when he appears in the doorway again with a glass of water. I ignore it and swallow my pill whole, almost choke, because I hate taking pills dry, and then reluctantly gulp the rest of it down with a glass of water.

"Give me your phone," I say crossly.

He hands it over wordlessly.

I hand it back because it's password-protected and glare at him.

He unlocks it, still without saying a word, and once again gives it to me.

Once I find Beck's number—what the *fuck?* They freaking *talked* earlier. My brother is *dead*—I program it into one of the burner phones, then surrender Wyatt's phone to him. "Thank you."

"You're welcome."

We're the most obnoxiously polite people in the world right now.

He stares at me a beat too long.

I stare back.

You're not a bad kisser.

"You're on the hook for playing my boyfriend all week," I inform him. "My *smitten* boyfriend who *adores* me. And don't try to get out of it. You *asked* for this when you ruined my plans with Grady."

"Fine."

"*Fine?*" What the hell? He's not going to argue?

"Yes. *Fine.*"

"I'm telling Beck."

"So he can blab to Monica that it's fake?"

Fucker. "So he doesn't freak out when he sees you grabbing my ass in any of Monica's photos."

He smirks. "So that's what you want from me."

"Yes, Wyatt. I want you to be a total Neanderthal and take me on every horizontal surface in Shipwreck, and then I want you to fondle me in public until we both get arrested for indecent exposure, because you're *so manly* and I *just can't resist the allure of your testosterone.*"

He smirks again. "Goodnight, Ellie."

I scowl, because he's not taking the bait, and I'm out of other ideas to annoy him. "Goodnight, Wyatt."

He snorts softly, which feels like him getting the last word, when he's probably making a not-so-silent commentary on *me* getting the last word.

I don't snort back. For the record.

Not until he closes the door anyway.

EIGHT

Wyatt

TUCKER and I are at the island in the kitchen, chowing on eggs, Mrs. Ryder's biscuits—god bless that woman for teaching me to cook—and bacon, debating if we're going to play miniature golf at Scuttle Putt first or go check out Davy Jones's Locker—Shipwreck's water park—when the doorbell rings.

We both look at the tablet hung under the cabinet, because everything around this house is wired with security cameras, including the doorbell. Half a biscuit falls out of Tucker's mouth. "Dad..." he whispers while I take in the muscled guy on the front porch with a bicycle leaning against his hip and a white bakery bag in hand. "That's Cooper Rock. *Cooper Rock came to see us.*"

"Yeah, bud, looks like he did."

While I'm sitting there growling to myself, wondering why a pro baseball player is dropping by at this hour of the morning, Tucker takes off like a shot, dashing to the door and flinging it open. "*Cooper Rock*! You came to see us! Can I have your autograph? Can we play catch? Can you *please* win today? I know you can win. You won a game just last week. You can do it again."

I put in the alarm code while it beeps in warning, then pull Tucker off the guy, who's grinning in amusement once again. "Gonna do my best, little man. You like donuts?"

"*Yeah*!"

"Have to save two for Ellie, but here, you can have the rest."

"Eggs first," I tell Tucker, rescuing the bag before he can make off with it and eat all seven pounds of donuts inside.

"But, Dad—"

"Go on. You were almost done anyway."

He looks back at Cooper. "Can you sign my arm?"

"How about a pirate sword?"

"*Yeah*!"

Cooper points to a sword on Beck's entryway table. "May I?"

I hand it to him. He pulls a Sharpie out of his back pocket and scribbles his name, then presents it to Tucker, who stares in awe.

"How's Ellie?" Cooper asks.

I cross my arms and study him carefully, because I don't care if he plays baseball or if he's a fucking priest, and I don't care how nice he was last night, I want to know if he has ulterior motives for asking. "Fine," I say shortly.

"She's still sleeping," Tucker offers.

Cooper clearly tries to swallow a grin, though I don't know which of us he's more amused by.

"She should be, the way she was dancing last night."

"She was *dancing*?"

"But don't worry. We helped her get up on the table and made sure she didn't fall down."

"You—"

"Man, you should see your face." He shakes his head. "She sat at the balcony table at Crusty Nut most of the night, then did the mini-golf course with her friends. But good to know she's in good hands." He slaps me on the shoulder and turns, straightening his bike as he flashes Tucker a grin. "Thanks for the support, little man. Stay strong, okay?"

My boy nods. "The Fireballs are gonna come back and win the World Series this time for sure! I've waited *seven years* for this."

"Yeah, I've waited *twenty*. And I gotta run, or I'm gonna be late getting back to the city for practice."

"Hit a home run!" Tucker yells, but I hear something else too.

Something that distinctly sounded like a woman yelling, "*Oh, fuck!*"

Somewhere beneath us.

I peek in the donut bag, which sends the heavenly aroma of fried dough and sugar wafting into the foyer, and I spy at least a half-dozen cake donuts smushed in there.

"Eggs," I remind Tucker, and while he slumps off to the kitchen, I open the door to the basement and head down.

The game room's open. Ellie's on a stool, muttering enough *fuck*s to make a pirate blush while she bangs on the controller on Beck's Frogger arcade game.

The pink in her cheeks and that stubborn set to her jaw make my dick twitch.

Kissing her in December wasn't a fluke.

Is she obnoxious? Yes. Short-tempered? Sometimes. Determined and smart and driven and fucking unstoppable?

Fuck, my pants are getting tight. Because there's nothing hotter than a woman taking charge and going after what she wants, and that's what Ellie Ryder has done every day of her life.

While thumbing her nose at me.

"Work work *work*, you son of a bitch," she growls.

"Donut?" I ask.

She throws a wild-eyed look over her shoulder. "*Frogger is broken.*"

I almost drop the bag, which would be a catastrophe, and not only because they smell delicious, but also because I'd have to clean it up. "What? No, it's not."

"*DO NOT TRY TO MANSPLAIN ME.*"

I growl while I cross past the ping-pong table, pool table, and foosball table to the far wall. "I'm not—what the hell is—dammit, Ellie, this is called *denial*, because Beck's gonna—oh, *fuck*."

The screen on the arcade console is one big squiggly mess of greens and blues. Ellie hits the buttons, and nothing happens. "I can't unplug it myself," she grumbles. "I can't fucking *bend* that way."

I toss the donuts on the ping-pong table behind me and shift behind the machine.

"Wait!" she shrieks.

"What?"

"Beck's high score. He'll kill you if his high score is gone."

I freeze.

She's right.

He hit seven hundred thousand something points over a weekend about two years ago. It was one of those rare times we were all around—Beck, me, the Wilson brothers, the Rivers kids, Davis, Ellie—and the whole weekend turned into one big party of watching Frogger and drinking beer and eating pizza and shooting hoops under the stars and just having fun again.

No worries, no responsibilities. Only *fun*.

Like when we were kids.

The whole crew will have a fit if that score's lost.

It would be like losing the weekend.

It's all we *did* that weekend.

"Can't you take out the screen and shake it and make it work?" she says desperately.

"It's not a fucking Etch-a-Sketch."

"But maybe it's the video card. Maybe if we get the video card out, we don't have to reset the whole system."

"Dad? Can I have a donut now?"

We both whip our heads around to look at Tucker, who's wearing a milk mustache and a yellow streak that I expect is egg down his Fireballs T-shirt, which isn't what he was wearing five minutes ago.

Also, did he just hear me say *fuck*?

Shit. I need to remember he can hear me. Bachelor life on base isn't good for a kid-friendly vocabulary.

"Yeah, bud. Help yourself."

Ellie's watching me with wide eyes, like she has an idea.

Like she's thinking nobody would say a word if Tucker spilled milk on the video game.

He's just a kid.

And it could be our secret.

And—

She breaks eye contact, shaking her head with a high laugh. "We are terrible people," she whispers. Then she shrieks. "No! Don't hit the reset button! Maybe we can unplug it without losing the high score, but reset will *definitely* erase it."

We're an hour and a half by car into Copper Valley. The city's our best bet for getting the system looked at, but just because it has a million residents doesn't mean a single one of them will specialize in fixing a vintage 1980's arcade game.

Beck said he had to go all the way to Atlanta to get this one.

"Two options," I tell her. "We call a repair guy, or we reboot and hope for the best."

"What if we can't save it at all?"

"Whatcha doin'?" Tucker asks. He's standing at the ping-pong table, donut in one hand, rubbing the top of a sparkly notebook next to it with the other.

"Mr. Beck's game broke. We're trying to fix it. Hang tight, bud. We'll go golfing soon, okay?"

"Okay," he replies around a mouthful of glazed donut.

"Did you go out for donuts at Crow's Nest?" Ellie asks. There's pure lust in her eyes. And her voice. And my dick notices.

"Cooper Rock biked up to drop them off for you."

She blinks at me.

Then blinks again.

And then she busts up laughing.

At *me*.

"Feeling inferior?" she asks.

"You want me to pull this plug?"

"No, I don't want you to pull the plug! I want you to fix it."

This is new, Ellie asking me for something. Usually she'd tell me to go away, that she'd do it herself.

We're like...a *team*. It's weird. But not unpleasant.

I yank out my phone and start googling, because if we're going to work together, I'm going to have The Google on my side before I do anything stupid.

"Look up if the high scores are erased if you unplug it," Ellie tells me.

"Who's mansplaining now?" I mutter, which earns me a light shove in the shoulder.

My skin tingles under my shirt, like I'm in danger of getting struck by lightning, and I concentrate on reminding myself that getting Ellie riled up is good for her, and has nothing to do with *me*.

Even if I did toss and turn half the night thinking about kissing her again.

"Alright, we shouldn't lose the high score if we reset it by pulling the plug," I tell her.

"But it's *old*," she points out. "Are you sure that's accurate for old machines?"

"You're right. We did just invent radio signals two years ago. I should check out this internet that's been around since the twentieth century some more."

"*Fine*, Mr. Expert. Pull the plug. But it's on you if the high score's lost."

"I wasn't the one who broke it," I point out.

"I *wouldn't* have broken it if—"

She cuts herself off sharply, pursing her lips and looking over at the Ms. Pac-Man game.

Was she about to say *if you hadn't kissed me*?

I don't remember who kissed who, but I'd take the blame.

It was worth it.

"Leg hurt too much to sleep?" I ask while I bend over behind the machine again and trace the right cord to the outlet.

"Yep."

"Huh. My lips bothered me all night. Probably need Chapstick. It's the elevation. Dries you out."

She doesn't answer, but she doesn't have to.

I'm getting her goat.

I can *feel* it.

Plus, I've been practicing since I realized I annoyed her when I was about thirteen.

I know how to shoot a basketball, Wyatt. I don't need you to show me how.

Damn if I didn't have some fun telling her she was doing it wrong just to see her face light up in independent indignation for the rest of high school. It was almost as good as having my own little sister.

Until it wasn't.

Because Ellie Ryder grew up, and she grew up stronger and faster and better at every sport she tried, and maybe it's ego, but I swear she wouldn't have been half as good if I hadn't goaded her.

And I noticed. Believe me, I noticed. Even when I knew I shouldn't, I did.

I yank the plug, and the fan inside the machine whirs to a stop. After counting to three, I plug it in again, then straighten to watch the screen.

Ellie's rubbing her thigh, and I wonder if it's aching this morning.

Not that she'd tell me if it was. She doesn't admit weakness.

Not if she can help it.

The game flickers to life, the screen back in normal operating mode, and I breathe a sigh of relief while Ellie sags next to me.

Close enough that she's almost sagging *into* me, matter of fact.

"Oh, *shit*," she whispers.

Tucker giggles.

"Watch your mouth," I mutter, but I realize she's gone pale. "What?"

She points to the screen.

To the top. Where it's supposed to say *HI-SCORE 701,400*, but instead says *HI-SCORE 0*.

"No, no, *no*," she groans. "Do you know what this means?"

"Beck's gonna kill you," I offer. Fuck, I've got sweat gathering at my collar, because Beck's gonna kill *us*.

Dating his sister might be okay—not that I have time in my life for that even if I'd let myself imagine it—but killing his Frogger score?

We're both dead.

But I can't say that to Ellie, because now I *have* to annoy her. It might be the only thing I do right for my buddy this week.

He spent hours. *Hours*. And we killed his high score. On his favorite game. *Fuck*, we all pitched in, egging him on, bringing him pizza. Levi even wiped his chin a few times so he didn't have to break from playing.

It's just a game.

This is stupid.

Except it's the memories. And the glory. And Beck's favorite game.

Tucker giggles again. "Daddy, what's a ball chain?"

"What's a what?"

"A ball—"

Before he can answer, Ellie's shrieking again. She leaps off the stool, almost goes down to her knees, but doesn't stop as she dives for the notebook in his hands. "Ohmygod, that's not for you!"

She snatches the notebook, but not before I see—a drawing of a short penis? And two boulders?

"I like Dick and his Nuts," Tucker says. "They're funny."

Her face is a cherry tomato with eyebrows and flashing blue eyes. "*Please* don't open random notebooks and sketchpads in this house. You don't know what you're going to find, and my brother has some *very* adult things that you shouldn't see."

Beck doesn't have notebooks and sketchpads.

Beck plays video games when he's here. Sometimes poker.

But he's never doodled or written stuff a day in his life.

Ellie, on the other hand…

"Not one word." She lifts her palm to me and hobbles out of the room, but not before grabbing the donut bag too. "Not a single word."

"Hey, you've got some Frogger to catch up on," I call after her. "Seven hundred thousand points worth."

She glances back at me, sees Tucker isn't watching, and lifts a middle finger.

I stifle a grin, because that attitude?

That's pure, classic Ellie Ryder.

And seeing her coming back in full force is more relief than I can ever admit to anyone.

Especially her brother.

NINE

Wyatt

TUCKER and I are on the eighteenth hole, after having survived leaving the house with Ellie insisting she didn't need a ride anywhere and that she'll make sure none of Beck's notebooks get left out again.

I smirked at her, letting her know I didn't believe her, and she flipped me another bird when Tucker's back was turned.

On the miniature golf course, we've made it past the English cannon attack hole, the mermaid hole, the hurricane hole, and more, to finally reach the Kraken hole. It seems wrong that we've come this far just to lose our balls to one of the sea monster's mouths—or possibly his eye sockets—but I guess that's the life of a pirate.

"Dad! Dad, I got it in his *nose*! Did you see?"

"You gave him a golf ball booger. Good job."

Tucker throws his arms around my waist. "I'm so glad you're my dad."

My sinuses get heavy and I blink a couple times before I hoist him up for a hug. Most days, I feel like I get more wrong than I get right, and I don't have a fucking clue what he'll think of me when he grows up—I'm supposed to be there for him *every day*, not just calling him at bedtime from Gellings Air Force Base five hundred miles away in Georgia—but he still seems to think I'm good at the dad job for now.

"I love you," I tell him.

"I know," he replies, and I set him down with a chuckle. "Your turn, Dad. I'll bet you can get it right in his forehead. That's the hardest shot, so they made the hole really big. I'll bet even Cooper Rock couldn't get it in his forehead."

I oblige and sink my ball into the Kraken's forehead, which, indeed, is the biggest hole. But I don't tell him that makes it the easiest, because I like being his hero.

"Someday, I'm gonna be a putt-putt master just like you," Tucker informs me.

I take his hand while we head over to turn in our clubs. "Someday, you'll be even better than me."

"Yeah, because I'm gonna be Captain America one day," he says sagely.

"Captain America? Who wants to be Captain America when you can be Blackbeard?" the wizened old man behind the counter says with a wink while we hand him our clubs. He's sporting an eye patch, a pirate hat, and a parrot on his shoulder.

"Fucking Blackbeard," the parrot says.

"Hush, hush, Long Beak Silver." The old pirate—pretty sure they call him Pop around here, head of the Rock clan—looks sternly at Tucker. "Don't ever let your grandkids parrot sit. They teach terrible words. But I'll get 'em. I'll get 'em all. I'm fixin' to set every one of 'em up with the love of their lives, and that'll teach 'em."

"Empty threats," a pretty woman in jeans and a Shipwreck T-shirt says as she strolls in the door. "If you were going to set us up, you would've done it by now."

"Maybe I should practice on this young man."

Tucker giggles again. "I don't want to fall in love with a girl. I'm only seven."

"Hmmm… Then maybe I should practice on your dad."

"He's in love with his work."

Pop and his granddaughter both cough, identical blue eyes

twinkling while I scrub my hand over my face to keep Tucker from seeing the irritation blossoming.

His mother shouldn't say things like that in front of him. I'm not *married to my work.*

I have split priorities between family and country. Whereas she—

Nope. Won't help. Not going there.

"Ah, a tough case," Pop says. "Good. It'll just prove to my grandkids that it can be done."

The woman rolls her eyes. "Have no fear," she tells me. "You're safe."

"You hungry?" I ask Tucker.

"I was hungry back before we jumped over the alligators, but they scared the hungry right out of me. I could be again though. Let me check." He pats his stomach. "Hey, belly, you want some food?" He cocks his head, then nods. "It says yes, Dad. We want more donuts."

We escape the matchmaking old man and head down the street to check out the wait at Anchovies, the pizza joint in the middle of Blackbeard Avenue. The hairs on my arms rise to attention a split second before I realize who's in front of us in line.

Ellie's best friend.

The bride.

She's in jeans today, but her T-shirt has a skull and crossbones on it, and she's wearing pirate boots and parrot earrings.

"Oh my gosh, it's Ellie's Wyatt," she says.

Fuck.

Dammit.

Small town. Guess it was bound to happen.

The two men and the woman with her all glance back at Tucker and me, and I instinctively grip his hand tighter while I nod to her. "Morning."

"We're not going to have to fight over who gets to sit with her, are we?" she asks.

The Blond Caveman goes stiff, earning a suspicious look from the redhead with him, but doesn't explain where Ellie is right now.

"I love Miss Ellie," Tucker declares. "She shares her donuts."

With some of us.

I didn't get any.

The bride—Monica, I'm almost positive, who Beck's mentioned a time or two, said she was Ellie's best friend since college—squats down to Tucker's level. "Do you want to sit with us so we don't have to fight over her?"

"Yeah! And I'll share my shaker cheese with her to thank her for the donuts."

"Perfect. Jason, sweetie, make it a table for seven," she tells the longer-haired blond holding her hand.

"We wouldn't want—" I start.

"Don't be silly. They have to push two tables together for a party of five anyway, so we're being more economical. Plus, who wouldn't want to eat with a kid this cute?"

Tucker grins up at me with his crooked, oversized front teeth, unruly brown hair, button nose, and dirty glasses, and I can't help smiling back.

I should object more, but it's likely me joining them for lunch will piss Ellie off.

And that *is* my secondary job for the week, right behind having fun with Tucker and right before losing sleep to try to recover Beck's high score on Frogger.

Oh. And that whole *playing her boyfriend* thing.

Which I intend to enjoy every minute of.

Just to watch her ex squirm.

If *he* hadn't pulled the dick of all dick moves—who dumps someone on *Christmas*?—she wouldn't have been at her parents' place looking for someone to share her misery with.

Easier to blame him the more I decide he's a turdnugget.

"How was the parade?" Monica asks Tucker.

"Where's Ellie?" Blond Caveman asks me while Tucker tells Monica he liked the parade.

I know his name, but I prefer to call him Asswipe. Since I can't do that in front of my kid, Blond Caveman it is.

"She's getting fitted for a peg leg," I tell him.

"Seriously, Patrick, I just told you," Monica says with a sigh.

"She's parking her car and fighting with Grady about accepting a ride in a golf cart."

"You didn't drive her?" Blond Caveman says.

"She wanted to not share the rest of her donuts, since Cooper Rock delivered them," Tucker announces. "He signed my pirate sword. I wonder if he signed one for Miss Captain Ellie too?"

"Cooper's signed *tons* of things for Ellie," Monica tells him. "But she doesn't usually keep them. She donates them to auctions for pet shelters."

"Like for dogs and cats?"

"And sometimes goats and snakes and hedgehogs."

Tucker frowns, like he's pondering a shelter for goats and snakes and hedgehogs.

"I *told* you I could walk," says a familiar voice that sets Dr Pepper buzzing through my veins.

We all turn as Ellie gives an exasperated sigh, then leans over to hug the Rock guy who was supposed to be her date last night. He's driving the golf cart that she's climbing out of. "But thank you."

"It's worth it just to watch you have to take help," he tells her with a flirty grin, and I consider how much more attractive he'd be with a broken face.

I scowl at him.

He catches my gaze and winks. "Got a live one there, bro. Lucky man."

"What is *with* all the men in my life being ass—uming blockheads?" she finishes as her gaze lands on Tucker.

"Hi, Miss Ellie!" Tucker calls. "Did you bring more donuts?"

"Not unless we're having pizza donuts for lunch," she replies. "Did you beat your dad in golf?"

"No."

"There's always next time. High five for trying." Her gait is stiff, but she's smiling at Tucker like she can feel no pain and she bends over to high-five him.

"Could you beat my dad in golf?" Tucker asks.

"Every time," she tells him.

"Because I let her," I add.

With a smile.

Like our relationship thrives on one-upmanship.

"And isn't that the sweetest?" she says tightly with a smile of her own.

"Miss Captain Ellie, I want a llama someday," Tucker declares.

Ellie gasps. "No way. Me too! Aren't they so cute?"

"I'm going to name mine Llama Llama Ding Dong because my teacher plays that song all the time."

"You—I—do you know you're freaking adorable?"

"Yeah."

He grins. She ruffles his hair, then moves in to greet Monica with a hug. When she's done, just to piss her off—and to watch the Blond Caveman fume too—I wrap an arm around her shoulders and kiss her flowery-scented hair.

I have a role to play.

I'll explain it to Tucker later. Shouldn't be too hard. *We're old friends.*

Not sure how I'm going to explain to my dick that we're not doing this for real again, but it'll live.

"Enjoy your ride?" I ask.

"Quit trying to help me walk. I can do it myself."

"I can help you walk, Miss Ellie," Tucker offers.

"Aww, that's so sweet of you, but I have to eat with—"

"All of us," I interrupt.

"We get to have lunch together!" Tucker says. "Captain Monica says so. Can you teach me to draw a—"

"Pirate?" Ellie exclaims desperately. "Yes. I can teach you to draw a pirate. Or a parrot."

"The golf man's pirate said a dirty word."

"Aw, Pop Rock's working at Scuttle Putt today? His parrot usually does say dirty words. He's a very salty bird."

Our table is called, and we head inside with Tucker proudly holding Ellie's hand. "Be careful, there's a chair," he tells her, steering her around one of the thick wood tables in the treasure-themed dining room.

"Thank you so much, gallant sir," she replies, then adds under her breath to me, "Why are you here?"

"Serendipitous timing. And fate, of course. I sensed you'd be here, and I missed you."

She looks at me closer, and there's a gleam in her eyes like she's gearing up to top me in the lovey-dovey new relationship game.

Which shouldn't be a big surprise. She's always been bright.

"Here, Miss Ellie. You sit on the end so you can put your foot up if you need to."

Tucker helps her gracefully into a chair—as gracefully as a seven-year-old who barely hits four feet tall can—and gives her a funny look when she replies, "Thank you, kind sir, you may kiss my hand."

"It's what gentlemen used to do for ladies," I whisper to him.

He wrinkles his nose at me like I'm asking him to hug an eel. "Dad, I like her, but I don't want to *kiss* her."

"Here. No cooties. Like this." I bend over, take Ellie's hand, and press a loud, smacking kiss to it, but I also trail my fingers down her palm.

Lightly.

Where no one can see.

Goosebumps visibly travel up her arm, and there's a tremor in her hand before I lower it, still holding on.

"See?" I say to Tucker. "Nothing to it."

I help Tucker into his chair on her other side and take the liberty of sweeping her short, dark curls back from her cheek before I pull out my own chair and sit.

Something squishes under my ass, and I register cold liquid on my left butt cheek the same moment a woman behind me shrieks.

I leap up as fast as I can, bumping into a passing server, who dumps a pizza all down the back of the woman who just got sprayed with—with *what*?

Whatever it is, it's red and sticky and why the *fuck* is there a bottle of ketchup in a pizza joint?

"Oh my god, you sat on the French dressing!" Blond Caveman's girlfriend says. Her eyes are round like she's both horrified and trying not to laugh.

"French—*what*?" Tucker asks.

"The French dressing," Ellie tells him, and I can hear her trying not to laugh as she scoots her chair, winces, and tries again to rise. "They put it on the pizza here, and—oh. Right. Bad time. Sorry."

"I'm so sorry. Oh my gosh, ma'am, I'm so, *so* sorry," the server is babbling. "Sir. I'm so sorry. I don't know how—why—"

I try to help her pick up the pizza. "My fault," I tell her. "Should've looked before I sat."

Ellie's sucking her cheeks in, face pointed at the ground. Tucker looks like he can't decide if he's supposed to laugh or cry.

"Daddy made a big boo-boo," I tell him.

"This isn't funny," Monica whispers, like she's talking to herself, while her face contorts with the effort of holding in laughter.

Her fiancé is on the ground helping me, lips twisted in a wry grin. "Could've happened to any of us, man. Ellie, sit. We got this."

A manager rushes over, and Blond Caveman's girlfriend leaps into action, checking the woman behind me for pizza burns. "I'm a nurse," she says, like she just remembered. "May I?"

"Wyatt?" Ellie whispers in a strangled voice.

"Yeah?" I grunt while I swipe at melted cheese on the old wood floor.

"I'm sorry you're having a shitty day."

All of a sudden, the woman we've accidentally assaulted with French dressing and pizza bursts into laughter. "What are the odds?" she says.

"I'm really sorry, ma'am," I say again.

"Honey, I was just sitting here mad because I have to go see my sister-in-law, who's always talking about all the terrible calamities that happen to her, like getting a wart on her knee, which is a pretty lame calamity, but that's my sister-in-law for you, and now I got a story that'll top her for life."

"Ma'am, we're still going to have to comp your pizza and give you a coupon for more. And a free T-shirt," the manager says.

"Can I get one of those glow-in-the-dark cups and a pirate mug too? I'll pay for it, but I'm telling her I got it all for free." She cackles as she rubs the French dressing on her shirt with a napkin. "She's gonna be so jealous."

"Her mug's on me," I tell the manager.

"I'll buy her an Anchovies hoodie," Jason pipes up.

"Put one of them squeezy treasure chests for her on my bill," a grandma two tables over calls. "This is the best entertainment I had since Blackbeard stripped for me two nights ago."

Half the people in the restaurant groan. "Didn't need to know that, Sandy!" someone calls back.

"There are kids in this place, Nana," the manager chastises.

"A stress chest? That's it?" someone else says. "Cheapskate. I'm getting a whole *set* of mugs for her."

"And I'm buying that table's dinner," another voice chimes in, pointing at us.

"Root beer all around!" someone hollers.

Despite sitting on French dressing for the next hour—the remains of which Ellie slathers all over her pizza and talks Tucker into trying too, after she's taught him how to draw a pirate face —lunch is just as much fun as Scuttle Putt was, except with more sea shanties and souvenirs. Monica's toned down the shrieking about Ellie and me *dating*, and instead is peppering me with questions about being a flight test engineer. Except for the occasional snide comment about my pay grade, the Blond Caveman keeps his attention focused mostly on his phone. Jason tells us all about the last time he went to Africa with the nonprofit he works for, and then brags on Monica's recycled artwork.

And Tucker gets to color a pirate ship that Ellie draws him on the paper placemat, which keeps him happy long after he's done eating. He's loaded down with more loot than he picked up at the parade by the time we leave.

"This town is crazy," I mutter to Ellie once we're back out on the street, stuffed with the best thin crust pizza in the entire state.

"Customer service and reputation above all else," she replies. "Welcome to the Shipwreck family."

Two pirates on unicycles are juggling back and forth right in the center of Blackbeard Avenue, and the Sea Cow Creamery across the street is handing out free samples to anyone willing to shout *Ahoy, matey!* to distract them.

Everyone's smiling despite the pirate insults flying.

Everyone except the Blond Caveman.

He's scowling at me.

And I'm ignoring him.

"You guys are coming with us to Cannon Bowl, right?" Monica says.

"Wyatt promised Tucker a trip to Davy Jones's Locker," Ellie says with just enough regret in her voice that I almost hope Tucker announces he'd rather go bowling.

He doesn't, of course.

Kid loves a good water park.

But I make sure to kiss Ellie goodbye before the bridal party departs. A good kiss.

The kind of kiss that suggests there's more waiting where that came from.

And fuck if I wouldn't kiss her longer if I could.

Blond Caveman glares at me.

And I decide I'll be perfectly content playing her *boyfriend* for the rest of the week.

"Dad, friends kiss, right?" Tucker asks as we head to the car for the swim bag and more sunscreen.

"Grown-up friends do sometimes, yes," I tell him.

"Does that mean you're getting married too?"

Fuck, I never should've gotten married the first time, but I thought it was the right thing to do. No chance in hell I'll do it twice.

I squat down to his level. "You know you're number one in my life?"

"Behind your job."

I shake my head. "I do my job to keep you and your friends and your friends' families safe. Because I love you first, even when my job keeps me away. I miss you every day. And I might have special friends come and go, but *you* will always be most important. Okay?"

He frowns like he wants to ask more, but just says, "Okay."

And once again, I wonder how much I'm messing him up.

But this is my life in the Air Force. I move. I make new

friends. They leave. I make more friends. Then I leave. It's the life a lot of military kids live too.

You have to say goodbye a lot, but you meet a hell of a lot of good people along the way.

I'll miss it when I'm done, which will be sooner than I ever wanted, but the odds of me having a long career in the Air Force close to Tucker are slim to none.

"We're pretty dang lucky," I tell him. "We got to share lunch with a bunch of people who think you're awesome."

He grins at me. "That's 'cause I am awesome, Dad."

He sure fucking is.

TEN

Ellie

I SPEND the rest of the day feeling weirdly lonely despite being with Monica and Jason.

Yes, and Patrick and Sloane too, but it's weird to hang out with a man I've seen naked, knowing he gets naked for someone else now, so I'm concentrating on my best friend instead.

And not on Wyatt.

That kiss.

Tucker and his sweet insistence that no one else could ever draw pirates like I could.

"The parents get here tomorrow," Monica tells me with a nose-wrinkle as we reach my car in the parking lot. She insisted on walking with me, and since we haven't had much alone time the last few weeks aside from driving out here, it's good to have a few more minutes of *us* time. "My mom still doesn't understand the pirate wedding thing, but I think when she sees Jason sword fight the mutinous pirates who want to steal me after we say our vows, she'll get it."

I laugh. "I love you."

"Of course you do. Everyone else you know is B-O-R-I-N-G." She gives a mock eye roll, and we both crack up again, because there's nothing remotely boring about the people I've known longest in my life.

Beck and half the guys we grew up with have been world famous since before I graduated high school, and it hasn't always been easy to find the true friends from the people who just want to get close to Beck and his Bro Code bandmates. But Monica's all country, all the way, and she always has been. She couldn't pick a boy band out of a lineup, and she'd rather drool over Orlando Bloom in *Pirates of the Caribbean* and Captain Hook from *Once Upon A Time* than check out my brother's Instagram page.

She also always asks me to turn the cardboard cutouts of him around whenever she stops by his house.

Or my parents' house after Beck's been there and left a few more.

He's such a goober.

"Seriously, though, I will completely understand if you beg off anything with Jason's parents. I sometimes wonder how he came out of the same gene pool as the rest of them."

"Every family has a black sheep." The Dixons' is Jason. He works for a nonprofit whose mission is to provide clean drinking water in third world countries, instead of going into the banking business with his father and brother.

Or even into the socialite business with his mother.

It's been long enough since Patrick and I broke up that I've finally been able to see clearly how my priorities have been messed up most of my life. I thought having a solid career, a stable husband in a complementary career, and adorable children to carry on the Ryder family environmental engineering firm was what it's all about.

But the idea of being one-half of a power couple doesn't appeal to me anymore.

And the more time I spend around Patrick, the more I question everything I ever wanted.

He spent half of lunch checking out his phone. He missed an entire two games of bowling for an important work call. And it wasn't until Sloane took his phone away at dinner that he finally engaged in a conversation that wasn't about his travel, clients, or work hours.

Or baiting someone. Like Wyatt at lunch.

The military? That doesn't pay very well, does it? Oh, that's right, you're divorced. I would never let my child go a week without seeing me.

When we were together, I thought he was charmingly cynical. Now, I can see he's truly an asshole in the way that makes Wyatt look like...not such an asshole.

And Patrick learned it from his parents.

"There's no way I'm making you face Jason's parents by yourself. I'll be there, and if they get snippy, I'll just mention how many of my other ex-boyfriends sent flowers after my accident."

Monica sighs. "They're just so oblivious sometimes."

I bite my tongue.

My brother is oblivious. The Dixons are just mean.

Except Jason.

Who's jogging into the parking lot now after stopping to help talk Pop Rock's cussing parrot off a roof. "Sorry, ladies," he says as he joins us. "Stubborn bird. How's the leg, Ellie?"

"Good." It's almost the truth, comparatively speaking. "You guys aren't going to The Grog without me tonight, are you?"

"Nope, we're saving that for tomorrow after our mothers drive us nuts," Monica replies happily.

Jason shakes his head, making his curls shake too. "They mean well," he tells her. He gives me a sheepish grin. "And I told mine to be nice to you."

"Don't worry about me. I've been through worse. You just enjoy your wedding week."

"Are you having fun?" Monica asks.

"Of course."

"Don't even try that with me. You're one degree of separation from needing to meet Willie Nelson for a joint. Do I need to talk to Wyatt about your need for backrubs and wine this week?"

"No, he's got that covered."

"So what's with the weird tension between you two at lunch? And don't tell me you were embarrassed about the dressing, because your brother models underwear for a living. Nothing short of full frontal exposure in public is grounds for *you* to get embarrassed."

Oh, fuck, she noticed? I drop my voice and try to come up with a reasonable explanation. "Tucker found my doodle pad this morning."

When the idea of a seven-year-old looking at Dick and the Nuts doesn't seem to faze her, I add, "While we were trying to fix Frogger."

"Holy shit, you broke Beck's Frogger?"

"Ssshhh! We're going to get the high score back," I say quickly. I have no idea *how*, but we will. "And did you miss the part about *my doodle pad*?"

"No, I'm trying really, really hard not to laugh at how Wyatt must've handled his son getting an eyeful of a penis cartoon. It's easier to do when I'm concentrating on the threat of your brother banishing you from ever using his weekend house again. Remember the time we snuck up here for my birthday party?"

"Oh my gosh, and all your friends from work?"

"And the poor shaved poodle?"

"And the stripper?" we say in unison, and we both double over laughing, which sends a jolt of pain to my knee, but fuck it, laughing feels too good.

"You had a stripper?" Jason asks mildly.

"A pirate stripper," I explain.

"A really *bad* pirate stripper," Monica adds.

"He tripped over his scabbard and accidentally mooned us trying to turn on his music."

"He was so cute."

"In a frat boy out of his element kind of way."

"We ended up getting him drunk and tutoring him in calculus."

"He still emails me his grade reports. I think he's graduating next year."

Monica's eyes dance. "He is? We should go to his graduation! Engineering school, right?"

"No, he decided political science was more his speed. His parents are crushed, but he's riding a 4.0 since he switched majors."

"We are *so* going to his graduation."

"It's a date."

"Hey, Ellie, you need a ride home?" Grady Rock calls from the edge of the makeshift parking lot.

"Got my car right here, but thank you," I call back, patting my white Prius.

"Still happy to give you a ride. My TV's out. Can't watch the game."

"Go crash Cooper's house."

"Pop's there."

"Go see your grandfather. It's good for your soul."

"Not when Nana's with him. They're disgusting. Heard she was telling stories at Anchovies about him stripping for her. Would you want to watch that?"

"We're going with her to make out on the couch," Monica tells him.

"Fucking hell," he mutters loud enough to carry. "Next time, then."

He waves good-naturedly and heads down the road.

"Aww, now I feel bad," she says. "Where's he going to watch the game?"

"His TV's not broken," I tell her. "He's just spreading that rumor so the rest of his family doesn't crash his place."

"Seriously?"

"Yep."

"How do you know all this?"

"Spend enough weekends in Shipwreck, you'll know what color underwear everyone wears too."

"What color underwear are you wearing today?" Jason asks Monica.

She grins at him. "Want to see?"

"Ack, not here." I shoo them both away. "Go on, go do your soon-to-be-newlyweds thing somewhere else. I'll see you at breakfast."

We pass around hugs, and I climb into my car for the drive up the mountain. The sky's still a hazy gray-blue, but the sun's dipped below the mountain ridge to the west and dusk is settling. I make it home without incident before darkness has fully engulfed the roads, and when I limp into the basement from the garage, I find Wyatt and Tucker snuggled on the basement couch watching the Fireballs game.

They're oddly adorable, odd in the sense that I shouldn't find anything about Wyatt adorable. He's a military man through and through, his body a machine, his mind sharp, his expectations high, his hair short.

But sitting there with his legs propped up on the coffee table and his arm tucked around a sleeping, bony little boy in pajamas and messy hair, he doesn't look like a military man.

He looks like a father.

Mortal.

Compassionate.

Vulnerable.

Holding his world.

A world I always wanted but might never have.

He glances up at me and shakes his head. "Hurting again?"

"No." It's habit to be a petulant ass around him, and I sigh, because now I'm frustrated with myself. "Yes."

"Sit."

I limp to the edge of the couch and sag into it, then dig into my purse for the over-the-counter painkillers I prefer to the prescription stuff.

He passes over a stainless steel water bottle, and I thank him politely.

Because I cannot use Wyatt as a punching bag.

I'm better than that.

Plus, my problems aren't his fault.

And I really do need to be able to pull off looking like one half of a happy couple in front of Patrick's parents tomorrow.

They're the worst, and they'll throw the sharpest darts.

I lift the footrest with the controller sitting in the couch's cupholder and look at the screen after passing Wyatt's water back. "Do I want to know who's winning?"

"Maybe if you're a Pittsburgh fan."

The inning comes to an end with the Fireballs striking out, and I wince as the score flashes on the screen. "Can't win them all."

"Still three innings to go."

Tucker snores, and a gentle smile softens the hard angles of Wyatt's face. I turn my attention to a commercial about jock itch. "Too much fun wore him out?" I ask without looking their way.

"He's an amateur."

A surprised laugh slips out of me, because *fun* and *Wyatt* aren't two things I usually put together.

Except they probably should be. *Anyone* who hangs out with my brother knows a thing or two about fun.

"I'm sorry about Patrick," I tell him.

He shifts, and I realize he's watching me, puzzled.

"For him being so rude at lunch," I clarify.

"Happens," he says with a shrug. "Not your fault."

"It was my fault I dated him," I mutter.

"True enough." The puzzlement fades into a frown. "Think I deserve to take some shit. I still haven't said I'm sorry for what happened. Six months ago. For making you upset enough to leave. But I am. Sorry, I mean. I didn't mean to hurt you."

I freeze for a half a second, because he's not supposed to say he's sorry. "Can't live in the past," I say quietly.

I should go check my phone to see if it's working yet, but I want to sit for a little bit longer first. Not for the company, I tell myself, but for the rest.

The game comes back on, and he shifts. "Before I forget…"

He holds out my phone.

A shiver rolls through me, because was the man reading my mind?

"It works, and I didn't prank call anyone."

I stare at the device stupidly for longer than I should before taking it. Our fingers brush like they did over ice cream at Christmas. I remember the feel of his lips against mine, and a flush heats my entire body. "Thank you."

He frowns. "You okay?"

And there's more stupid staring going on as I blink blankly at him, because there's something in his tone that's not quite normal.

"You didn't yell at me for not letting you do it yourself," he clarifies.

"Twenty-something years of yelling at you hasn't worked, so

maybe it's time I give it up."

He shifts to lean over and touch the back of his hand to my forehead. Tucker grumbles in his sleep, but doesn't wake up.

"Yep, definitely warm," he says. "You should probably strip."

"Ex*cuse* you?" I gasp.

He grins. "Ah, there she is. Just checking."

"You're *trying* to annoy me?"

He looks down at Tucker, glances at the game and winces as Pittsburgh gets a double off what should've been a single, then looks back at me. "You remember we used to play basketball at the Rivers house?"

"I remember you used to think I couldn't keep up."

"You couldn't, but that's not the point."

My breathing is coming easier as we slip back into the old habits. "You are *so* lucky that innocent child is sleeping on you right now, or you'd be dead."

"I used to wait until you'd sink the *perfect* shot, and then I'd tell you that you could've done it better, just to watch the steam roll out your ears. And it's still that easy."

I gape at him, because *he does it on purpose*?

And what does it say about me that I still take the bait?

"You-you're—you're an *ass*," I gasp.

Tucker stirs, and I slap a hand over my mouth.

Wyatt just shrugs, but not the shoulder that would disturb Tucker. "I have to have some flaws. Otherwise I'd be insufferable."

That is *not* the guy who's been Beck's best friend for over twenty years. I narrow my eyes at him, but I don't call him on it. Because I have the oddest feeling that's exactly what he wants me to do.

But I can't resist asking, "Why only to me?"

He holds my gaze longer than I expect. "Because I was so fucking tired of being coddled, and you gave it right back, every time."

Just because I don't know what he's talking about doesn't mean he's not telling the truth. And there's a truth so clear in the ring of his words that I get a bone-deep shiver.

"Who coddled you?" I ask.

He shakes his head with a snort. "Better question is *who didn't?*"

"Why?"

He glances at the TV, and just when I think he's not going to answer, he does.

"Last guy my mom dated before she finally realized what she was doing to both of us and moved in with my grandma to reboot her life was a first-rate asshole," he says. "Let's leave it at that. But it meant my gran went around the neighborhood looking for any parents who had enough control over their kids to make them look after me."

"Beck didn't coddle you."

"At first he did. All of them did. I might've been small and damaged, but I wasn't blind."

My heart's starting to hurt, because *no* kid should *ever* feel damaged.

"Didn't mean I could take care of myself though. That I didn't need it. Wasn't big enough for that." He shakes his head. "Thought I could. But I couldn't. And Beck saved my ass when I got into it with his best friend. Could've left me behind. Instead, he dropped him. Hard. Broke his nose. Got a detention in sixth grade. And then he thanked me for showing him what a douche Andy Brentwood was. Dude all but saved my life and thanked *me* for it."

I swallow hard. I remember Andy, vaguely, but I never gave any thought to why Beck stopped talking about him. "That's not coddling you. That's doing the right thing."

"I started it. He got detention. I got chocolate chip cookies and milk. From your mom. From Mrs. Rivers. From my grandma. I shared so the Wilsons would teach me to lift weights and so Davis would teach me his Tae Kwon Do moves. I didn't want to be fucking helpless."

The groan of the crowd carries through the television, even at low volume, and I glance at the game, almost relieved by the distraction.

I had no idea I'd been being an asshole to a kid who'd had enough asshole in his life.

And that doesn't make me feel any better about my life choices.

Two-run homer. Fireballs are down by six now.

In the fifth inning.

It's going to be a blood bath.

Copper Valley's home team has never won a World Series, but they've never been quite as bad as they are this year either.

Even with Cooper Rock and his unbelievable gymnastics at second base.

"I always appreciated that you didn't cut me any slack, and I admired your determination," Wyatt says, speaking so softly I half think my ears are playing tricks on me. "If you could be that determined, then I could damn well be that determined too."

When I glance at him, he's still staring at the game.

But I know he said it.

And I know he knows I heard.

He settles deeper into the reclined seat at the other end of the couch. Tucker sighs and snuggles closer to him.

Little Tucker, safe, happy, and loved.

I overheard Wyatt telling Beck once, about eight years ago, that he didn't want to be a dad. He didn't know how. He was going to fuck it all up, and it wouldn't just be himself, it would be him and a wife and kid.

But Tucker?

That kid is so very, very loved. With two parents who might live in different states, but still happy. Well-adjusted. And *loved*.

And I realize I need to go.

Not so I can check my email and any messages that came in while my phone was drying. Not so I can call Beck and give my brother grief for sending Wyatt here during Monica's wedding week.

No, I need to go before I start seeing Wyatt as the man I glimpsed the night we hooked up in my parents' basement six months ago.

The angry father who just wants to be with his son.

Because *that* man is dangerous to my heart.

ELEVEN

Wyatt

THERE'S EXACTLY one sound that I will move heaven and earth to stop, and that's the sound of my son in pain.

Except as I sit here with Tucker sleeping peacefully on me, listening to Ellie limp up the stairs, I want to tear something in half to make *her* pain go away too.

I shouldn't. We're not exactly the enemies we were as kids, but we can't be much more than casual friends, or one of us will start wanting something the other can't give.

And she won't be the one unable to hold up her end of making something work.

No, that would be all me.

I hear every step as she makes her way slowly from the kitchen to the bedroom upstairs. Not because she's walking loudly. Not because there's a lack of insulation. But because I'm listening for it. When the distinct sound of running bathwater carries through the pipes behind the walls, I get hard as a brick.

She's taking a bath again.

And there's nothing I can say to my dick to convince it she's getting wet and naked for therapy and that there's nothing *sexy* about her soaking in a tub of hot water and bubbles.

I don't have enough fingers to count the number of times I've heard someone say Ellie's annoying, or god knows, the number of times I've thought it myself in my lifetime, but at Christmas, and again now, I'm getting pissed thinking about it.

She *is* smart. She *is* brave. She *is* strong. She *is* determined.

Why does that have to translate to *annoying*?

Why does she have to be disparaged for *wanting* something and going after it?

She's not power-hungry. She doesn't tear people down. She just wants her own bar set higher, and she doesn't apologize for it.

I force myself to sit through the rest of the game, which is painful more for knowing Ellie's upstairs naked than it is for watching the blowout. Tucker doesn't wake up when I carry him upstairs and tuck him into the queen-size bed that makes him seem even smaller, and my heart lurches even though I know he's getting the childhood every kid deserves, safe, happy, and loved, despite the hiccup with me not being able to leave Georgia to join him in Virginia yet.

He's not growing up hiding in shadows.

He has a capable mom who takes good care of him when I can't.

He's not me.

And I'm sure as fuck not any of the sorry excuses for human beings my mom used to date.

I should go to bed too, but I'm restless, and I want a snack, so I creep softly downstairs. I expect Ellie's in bed, but I hear her voice drifting down the hall when I get to the kitchen. "Don't even try to play innocent. You did this on purpose."

I swallow a grin, because it doesn't take a rocket scientist to know who she's talking to, and I'm not surprised to hear the echoes of Beck's voice, even though I can't make out the words.

None of my business—he can tell her whatever story he wants, and she won't believe him, because she shouldn't—so I dig into the fridge instead.

The same carton is sitting there, right in front, calling my name, just like it has been since I spotted it yesterday.

A take-out carton of banana pudding from Crusty Nut.

Ellie would probably kill me if I ate it.

There's a line between annoying her and going too far, and I can't decide which side of the line eating her leftover banana pudding would fall on.

On the one hand, it's not a donut. On the other, it's still banana pudding.

"He has a *what*?"

The surprise and sudden hush in her voice makes me pause.

"You're lying," she says. "Because it doesn't make any sense. He freaking *carried* me to my room last night."

And now I'm interested.

I grab the banana pudding, pop the lid, and snag a spoon and meander down the hallway. Beck's voice gets clearer.

"—undiagnosed cardio-telepathy-rhymmeria. He's being fucking stubborn and refusing to admit something's wrong, so we need you to be extra nice to him. And watch out for his kid too."

"Rymmeria? What's a—Beckett Ryder, so help me, if you're lying to me—"

"Ellie, it's three in the morning here, I have a ten-hour plane ride tomorrow, and I'm talking about one of my best friends. Do you think I'm lying to you?"

"Yes." There's a hint of doubt in her voice.

Beck grunts in frustration. "You really want to take that chance? If he has a heart attack on your watch, you're going to feel like an asshole for the rest of your life. He might even get kicked out of the Air Force."

I knock and don't wait before pushing the door open. Ellie gapes at me wide-eyed from the bed, holding her phone out in front of her. "What the fuck are you—do you have a heart condition—*is that my banana pudding*?"

She starts to leap, winces, looks down at her white tank top that leaves little about her nipples to the imagination, and pulls the covers up to her neck. "You are *dead*," she tells me.

I cross the room to lean into the screen on her phone, which puts me right in the sweet spot to have Ellie's dark hair tickle my face while whatever fruity bath crap she used tonight fills my senses.

Beck grins on the other end of the video call. "Wyatt, buddy, how you doin'?"

"A heart condition?" I say.

"Ellie was all we had on short notice to watch you, but you're gonna pull through." He winks, his blue eyes the same as Ellie's, though his face is sharper and his hair weirdly more styled. "Hang in there. More help's on the way."

"We beat your high score in Frogger," Ellie growls at the phone.

Beck's eyes go round. "The *fuck* you did."

"We did," I agree. "Ellie ditched wedding stuff all day today to cook for me, and Tucker kept running to refill my Dr Pepper."

"Prove it, motherfuckers."

"Maybe tomorrow. I'm tired, and we didn't get any sleep last night," Ellie replies.

"You two couldn't get along well enough to tie a shoelace."

We make eye contact, and I don't have to know what she's thinking to know that I'm thinking the same thing.

What's the one thing worse than ruining his high score?

We move in sync like we've planned this, and suddenly I have my fingers threaded through the loose tendrils of her curly hair to cradle her scalp while she fists my shirt at the collar and pulls me to her mouth, still holding the phone out in front of us.

I don't know if I'm kissing her or if she's kissing me, but our tongues are clashing just like they did at Christmas, and her sweet taste is the perfect complement to the lingering banana pudding flavor in my mouth, and she's making whimpery moaning noises that might be real or might be for show but I don't care, because *fuck*, this feels good.

So damn fucking *good*.

Just like it did six months ago.

"QUIT FUCKING MY SISTER'S MOUTH, YOU ASSHOLE!"

Fucking *hell*, I don't want to. But Ellie starts to pull away, so I let her go. She smiles sweetly at Beck, holding the phone close enough to her face that I'm not in the picture anymore. "We *totally* beat your Frogger score," she informs him.

He's glaring at her, jaw flapping like he wants to say something.

"Also, I think I'd know if Wyatt had an undiagnosed heart condition. Especially after what he did to me this morning."

I start to talk, because isn't *undiagnosed* kind of hard for *anyone* to know if *I* don't even know it?, but she holds up a hand, and since I don't actually want to give her a reason to notice another condition that kissing her makes me suffer from, I shut my mouth.

"You—" he starts.

"Goodnight, Beck," she finishes sweetly. "I have to go do...something."

She hangs up the phone and flings it on the bed, then grabs the banana pudding that somehow ended up on the nightstand. "Thank you for delivering dessert. You may go."

I watch her for a minute, and when she looks at me, the craziest thing happens.

We both start to grin.

"Davis," we say together, and it's suddenly a race to see who can call him first.

There's no telling if he'll answer—there's a lot I'll never know about Davis Remington, despite living next door to him for half my childhood—but if he can't do what we need, he'll know who can.

My call goes to voicemail, and I start talking two seconds before Ellie does. "Dude, it's Wyatt. Call me. It's about Frogger."

"Davis, it's Ellie. Beck's on my shit list and you owe me one for you know what, so get your ass up here to Shipwreck yesterday."

She hangs up and pulls the banana pudding out of my reach. "Don't even think about it."

"What does Davis owe you for?"

"Sexual favors."

My blood pressure goes past red to black. "The fuck he does."

"Why did you kiss me?"

Of course she won't shy away from asking. "So Beck knows there's something worse than losing his high score in Frogger. Why did you kiss me?"

"Because you're a good kisser."

Of everything she could've said, that's the last thing I expected.

But it shouldn't be.

It's Ellie. She charges in like a bull, fucks up, adjusts, and then hits it out of the park.

She's fucking unstoppable.

"That's not all I'm good at," I tell her, and I think that damn frog from the game is sitting on my vocal cords, because that came out way huskier than it was supposed to.

Like a promise instead of a threat.

"I'm aware," she says, equally throaty, but also equally tentative.

If that was all she said, I could walk away. But she adds, "I don't hate you, you know," in a soft whisper, and I sink to the bed next to her, because I'm pretty sure that was an invitation.

"And if you *were* suffering from a real heart condition, I would help you," she continues, softer still.

It's like Christmas all over again, hiding out in her parents' basement after finding out I lost the battle to keep Tucker in Georgia with me while I waited for orders to Copper Valley.

"You'd make a terrible nursemaid," I say hoarsely, because someone has to stop us from doing what I'm thinking of doing every time she lets her gaze drift to my lips like that.

"You'd make a terrible patient."

"I should leave."

"Why did you tell Beck you were going to make a terrible husband and father?"

Fuck, how did she know that? "Listening in on people's private conversations, nosy-ass?"

"Don't get high and mighty with me. I know you too well."

"Ellie—"

"Was I that much of a mistake? At Christmas?"

"No. Yes. Fuck." I rub a hand over my eyes. "The guys—your family—they're all the family I have left. Them and Tucker. I don't want to fuck that up."

"Do you honestly believe any of my family would put up with you if you weren't good enough for all of us?"

"Don't be nice to me."

"What if we *were* nice to each other?" she whispers.

"Ellie—"

"Shut up, Wyatt. I'm not asking for a relationship. I'm asking for a *friend*. I don't *want* to go to Monica's wedding by myself. I don't *want* to feel broken. I want to dream again. I want to know I can be *normal* again. I want to believe in the future. I can't—I haven't—I don't know if I can—"

She stops with a growl of frustration. "Never mind. Forget it. I—"

I have my hands in her hair again before I can think, kissing her hard and ruthless and unapologetically.

The last thing she did before her accident was, well, *me*.

If she needs help getting back in the saddle, then I guess the least I can do is, well, *her*.

Whatever she wants. As far as she wants to go.

That's what you do for a friend, especially a friend you didn't realize you needed until it was almost too late.

Right?

TWELVE

Ellie

SOMETHING THIS STUPID should not feel this right, but *dammit*, when Beck told me Wyatt had heart problems—even when I didn't believe him—my own nearly stopped beating.

Until Christmas, Wyatt was the annoyance from my childhood. But he grew up.

I grew up.

And then I stumbled into my parents' basement with a carton of ice cream, and now I'm back with the last person who saw me before I wasn't *me* anymore.

And he knows it, or he wouldn't be here.

He wouldn't stay, pretending to be my boyfriend with history hovering at the edges of the tension between us.

He tastes like banana pudding and feels like forgiveness, and if I think about this too long, I'm going to chicken out, so instead, I toss the pudding on the other side of the bed and give in to the sensations of his mouth, his lips, his breath, his grip on my hair, the hard plane of his chest against the extra fluffiness mine's acquired this year.

"Tell me to stop," he murmurs when he pulls out of the kiss to lick a path along my jaw.

"I'll kill you if you stop."

"Sweet talker."

"My nipples are hard."

"Fuck, Ellie. I can't—I'm not—you deserve—"

"Shut. Up." I'm drenched between my legs, and I can feel my pulse in my clit. "I know who you are."

He nips at the tendon between my neck and shoulder, and I grip his solid shoulders to hold him where it feels good. "More there," I beg.

He nips again, then licks at my sensitive skin, and I shift on the bed to carefully part my legs while he gently swipes my hair to the side, his fingers brushing the back of my neck and making me whimper in pleasure.

"There too?" he asks, rubbing his thumb at my nape.

"Mm-hmm," I manage.

"Relax, Ellie."

"I don't know how to relax. I was born this way. Take your shirt off."

"You first."

If he thinks I'm going to balk, he can think again. I whip my tank top over my head and let him see all of me. The fuller breasts. My tight nipples. The scars that are barely noticeable on the side of my left breast now.

He traces them anyway, because of course he notices, watching my chest with dark, hooded eyes. "Where else?" he asks hoarsely.

"Lose the shirt," I rasp out.

His eyes lift to mine, and there's raw hunger that I've never seen there before. Instead of ripping off the cotton shirt, he lifts it slowly, inch by inch, revealing the chiseled abs, the flat pecs, copper nipples pebbled hard, his arms flexing when he finally pulls it over his head.

"Show-off," I whisper.

"Look who's talking," he replies, bending to suck one of my nipples into his mouth.

Pleasure rockets from my chest to my core, starting that long-forgotten spiral of need deep inside me.

I forgot how big his hands are until he cups my other breast, fully covering it despite the two cup sizes I've gained. While he suckles harder on one nipple, he circles the other with his thumb. I arch into his touch. "Oh, god, yes," I moan.

I'm so damn glad he doesn't have a heart problem.

"Lie down," he says gruffly, pushing me with his body until I'm on my back, head on the pillow, the covers low on my belly. He starts to pull them off, but I grip them tight.

"Not yet."

He replies by moving to suck on my neck again while his hand slips under the covers and over my panties.

I part my legs more, and he dips his fingers between them over the thin cotton barrier. "Fuck, Ellie, you're soaked," he moans.

"Touch me, Wyatt."

He covers my mouth with his again, his tongue gliding against mine, his hard body pinning me down, one hand stroking my hair while his fingers slip under my panties to trace my seam.

We both groan into the kiss, and I suck hard on his tongue when he slides one digit inside me.

He moves slowly, carefully, while I test arching my hips into his touch. "More," I whimper.

"You are so fucking hot."

We dive back into the kiss while he adds another finger. I reach between us and fumble with the button on his shorts. When I finally reach inside and wrap my hand around his solid cock, he jerks his fingers hard inside me, reaching that desperate, aching, needy spot deep inside. "There," I gasp, squeezing him harder.

"Christ, Ellie, that feels good."

"Deeper, Wyatt, right—*oh, god, right there.*"

I pump him faster while he drives his fingers deeper. I lift my right knee to give him a better angle, jerking on his cock and tightening my grip until—

Until the tickle.

The tickle behind my left eyelid.

"Oh—ah—no—ahh—"

"Come for me, Ellie," he pants. "Fuck, I can't—you need to—you can do it—"

"Wya—ah—ahh—"

"That's it, baby. That's—"

"*Ah*-CHOO!"

My orgasm explodes, and pain explodes in my nose as the sneeze rockets through me and my head collides with Wyatt's. Something hot and wet squirts up my breast and into my armpit, and Wyatt grunts out a *fucking hell* before leaping back, covering his cock with one hand and his eye with another while he dashes to the bathroom, his shorts falling to his knees.

My eyes are stinging, my nose throbbing like someone's hammering a nail into it, and my pussy is still having orgasm aftershocks like it's no big deal that I just *sneezed all over Wyatt and head-butted him in the middle of a heavy petting session.*

I sneeze again, pain shoots through my entire face, and I stifle a whimper.

"I'm sorry," I call weakly.

Wyatt reappears in the doorway with his shorts back on and a fuzzy gray dog in his hand. I think. My vision's a little blurry with all the heat in my eyes, and I don't know where a fuzzy gray dog would've come from.

"Are you okay?" he asks.

"I'm sorry," I babble again. "Did I hurt you? I'm sorry. I didn't mean to—I didn't realize—that's only happened one time before—"

"Didn't need to know that," he mutters.

He rubs a towel—not a fuzzy gray dog—over my chest and side, and I realize he was in the middle of his own orgasm when I gave us both broken faces.

"Am I bleeding?" I whisper.

"No."

"Is your eyeball okay?"

"Yep."

"Um…thank you for the orgasm. It was very nice." Oh, *fuck.* I'm going to have a swollen nose for Monica's wedding. I'm going to ruin her wedding pictures.

Then I remember this is Monica, and she'll spend the rest of her entire life telling people I helped beat off the pirate vagabonds who tried to kidnap her from Jason at the wedding, and I even have the bruised nose to prove it, and I snort out a laugh.

And then I whimper in pain, because snorting and broken noses don't mix.

"Fucking hell, Ellie," Wyatt mutters. "We have issues. Can you walk? How's your leg? Get up. You can sleep in the guest room. I'll clean this up tomorrow."

He's still holding his eye while he finishes wiping me off.

"Are you sure your eye's okay?"

"Yes. Go on. You can't keep going on no sleep."

"I can clean this—"

He stands, plants his fists on his hips, spreading those shoulders even wider and holy banana pudding, the man could probably crack a walnut with those ab muscles.

He clears his throat. Oh, right.

He's glaring at me. "I'm aware you're perfectly capable. And I'm going to clean this, including the banana pudding, and you're going to go to sleep anyway. Say *thank you, Wyatt*."

I glance over and realize there is, in fact, banana pudding spilled all over the comforter.

"Thank you, Wyatt," I mutter with a sigh as I silently mourn the lost dessert.

"Are we done arguing now?"

"Are we ever?"

His lips twitch again, and *dammit*, now I'm on the verge of smiling too, despite the pain still radiating out of my nose.

"Make you a trade," he says suddenly.

"Why do I not trust you?"

"I'll let you clean this up tomorrow if you show me that notebook you took away from Tucker this morning."

I scurry out of the bed as fast as my leg will let me go. "*Fine*. I'm going. But if this swells up and bruises, I'm telling people I tripped while saving Tucker from a rabid coyote."

"And I'll tell them you threw a log at me when I tried to help."

"Perfect."

Before I can limp out of the room, he snags one of my hands. I glance up at him, suddenly aware that I'm standing here in nothing but my bare breasts, soaked panties, and the mangled scar on my left leg.

But he doesn't look down.

Nope, not Wyatt.

He simply presses a kiss to my forehead. "Friends?"

"Can I still tell you not to tell me how to do things?"

"And definitely give me your wrong opinions when I'm doing something not your way."

I ignore the sarcasm. "Only if you agree to do the same."

He snorts softly, and I'm pretty sure it's a snort of laughter and not utter and complete frustration. "You're one of a kind."

"And thank god for that. Beck would never keep up if there were two of me."

I swear he's smiling when I leave the room.

Mostly because I'm not sure my ego could take the hit if he was vehemently agreeing with my awful attempt at a joke.

THIRTEEN

Wyatt

THE SOUND of the house alarm buttons being pushed wakes me from a dead sleep at 4:30.

Someone's breaking in.

I fly out of the bed and land on soft feet, and I don't bother pulling on a shirt, because it's not going to be any protection against an intruder. I hit the bottom of the stairs when the lights flicker on, blinding me.

"Freeze, asshole!" Ellie barks. Something whizzes past me and thuds against the door.

The dark figure next to the alarm panel sighs. "A guy drives all night to answer a distress call, and what does he get? He gets a dildo launched at his face. Nice, Ellie. Real nice."

"*Davis*?" she shrieks.

The slender, man-bun-wearing, bearded *intruder* bends over and grabs the massive purple *thing* from the floor. It's longer than his tatted-up arm. "Fucking hell, does that even fit? Put your fists down, Wyatt, it's not about her honor. You see the size of this thing?"

Ellie snatches it back, but once she has it, she grabs it by the base with her other hand and wipes the first one on her shirt.

"Go put pants on," I hiss at her.

"It's like a swimsuit, Morgan," she snaps back. "And this isn't mine. It was in the drawer in the guest bedroom."

All three of us momentarily stare at the two-foot-long, six-inch-thick dildo dangling from her fingers. I try not to look at the mangled, leathery scar on her thigh, but my stomach still dips thinking about what she's been through.

"You should mount it," Davis says, nodding to the dildo.

Ellie goes stiff like she's going to beat him with it, and I'm about to slug him when his lips twist in a familiar smirk.

"On Beck's bedroom wall," he finishes.

His dark eyes flit between us. "And you two should be more careful when you're having sex. Looks like you had a threesome with a boxer."

Ellie's eyes bug out.

"We weren't—" I start, yanking my hand away from where it instinctively went to test the tender skin around my eye, but Davis pops a rare full grin and turns to the door to the basement.

"What'd you do to fuck up Frogger? And where's the coffee? If I'm gonna fix this, I need fuel."

"Screen went out, so we pulled the plug to reboot." I jerk my head back at Ellie. "*Please* go put pants on before Tucker comes down here and sees you walking around like that, because he'll tell his mother and I'll never hear the end of it."

I can deal with the guilt of seeing her scars.

But I really don't want Tucker thinking about women in underwear any younger than hormones finally make him.

"And don't forget my coffee, wench," Davis calls.

"Oh, go cut your hair," she replies good-naturedly with a smile.

She heads to the kitchen, swinging the dildo of indeterminate source, and I'm pretty sure she's going to at least wrap it in a garbage bag, if not take it all the way out to the trash herself.

I follow Davis into the basement. He was the youngest in our group growing up—of the guys, so excluding Ellie—the slowest to warm up to people, and he was the first to want to call it quits on the boy band thing. I don't know exactly what he does for a job now, but I know it involves computers, coding, and the nuclear reactor a couple hours south of here.

"Should've told us you were coming. We would've left the light on."

"Three calls in an hour, and you thought I wouldn't come?"

"Three?"

He smirks again. "I don't know what you told Beck, but he wanted photographic proof that his score's still the highest."

"I kissed Ellie. On video call with him."

"About fucking time, dude."

"Shove it, Remington. Not going there."

He flips on Frogger and whistles low. "You wiped it."

"Can you write a new high score on it?"

He gives me a *don't be a dumbass, of course I can* look. "Gonna take donuts and coffee. Wouldn't mind pretty company."

I spread my arms. "I'm free until my kid's up."

"How'd Ellie break it?"

"Maybe I did it."

"Dude. If it was your kid, you would've just told Beck. If it was you, you would've just told Beck. If you're calling me to fix it, it was Ellie. Man up and do something about it already."

Easy for him to say.

He has a career—and a bank account—that mean he doesn't move every one to four years unless he wants to. He doesn't have an ex-wife and a son to take care of, and no idea what he's going to do to support them if he has to leave the military next summer because of orders anywhere *but* Copper Valley. And he doesn't have a clue how ill-prepared I feel to be a good partner to anyone, let alone my best friend's sister.

Help her heal?

Yeah. I'm in.

Anything more than that?

I'm not the man for the job.

FOURTEEN

Ellie

"OH MY GOD, WHAT HAPPENED?" A human-size tropical bird—I mean, Monica rushes to join me outside The Muted Parrot, Shipwreck's bright, cheerful coffee shop, four hours after Davis made his unexpected appearance Wednesday morning.

"One of Beck's friends showed up in the middle of the night," I tell her. "I didn't get much sleep."

"Because he gave you two black eyes?"

"*Oh*! Oh. That. No, that was me walking into a cabinet door."

"*You had sex with Wyatt!*" Monica whisper-shrieks like I didn't just give her a perfectly reasonable explanation that had *nothing to do with having sex with Wyatt*. She claps her hands, and her fake red, yellow, and blue feathers all flap up and down with her as she bounces. "I *knew* it. I knew you weren't fake-dating him just to make Patrick quit acting all superior."

Oh, *shit*, I'm totally transparent.

"Of course I'm not," I whisper back. "I sneezed right as I hit the big O and we knocked heads and I can never have sex with him again."

She looks around.

I do the same.

Because I really, *really* shouldn't have said that.

However…it will be a *great* reason to break up with Wyatt at the end of the week. No blame. Just the simple truth that it's dangerous for us to be together.

There's no sign of Patrick anywhere—yes, I continue to worry he'll realize I'm a loser who's still not dating—which probably means he's on a work call. I wonder if Sloane's bored out of her mind, or if she's taken to mindlessly playing Treasure Hunter on her phone like I used to when I was waiting on Patrick to end one of his important work calls so we could go somewhere.

Some days I get really pissed at myself for not seeing the signs sooner that he didn't check the box for *good husband material*, even if his resume did. I like to think he changed while we were dating, that he wasn't always a workaholic tool, but what does that say about my influence and our relationship?

You drive men to work too hard so they can avoid you.

Lovely.

Monica pulls me into the coffee shop. She lifts two fingers for the barista, who doesn't bat an eye at getting a sign language order from a parrot, and she points at the back table, then drags me around the seashell-themed room until we're in the sun room at the rear of the restaurant.

Cautiously, it should be noted, but she's still dragging me over.

We have to look crazy, even in Shipwreck. Me in a knee-length denim skirt and a different Jolly Roger T-shirt from yesterday, as requested, and her dressed like a five-and-a-half-foot-tall parrot. I'm pretty sure the costume is just to annoy Jason's parents, but not completely sure.

I'm also impressed that she went through with it. I thought she was kidding when she showed me the costume online.

"Do we all get parrot costumes?" I ask as she pulls out a seat and points a wing, gesturing me to sit.

"No, I got you a monkey costume. Explain to me exactly why you think you can't have sex with Wyatt."

"We'll both end up dead."

She makes a *go on* gesture, like being dead isn't reason enough to not have sex. It also makes her beak flop around her head, and her brightly-colored feathers all dance with the motion.

I lean in close and lower my voice. "The first time we had sex, I had my car accident. We...messed around a little two nights ago"—yes, yes, it was just a kiss, but I'm warming up to this story—"and Beck's Frogger game died mere hours later. We were in the middle of *you know* last night, and I sneezed and gave us both black eyes. *We are not supposed to have sex.* I can take a hint from the universe."

"Wait. You said this happened mid-orgasm? Like, you got off, so the sex couldn't have been *bad*."

Bad? It was so far the opposite of bad that I don't have a word for it.

And that was just his fingers.

I might burst into flames if we ever went farther.

"Ellie! You're seeing someone? That's fantastic." Libby Rock, the middle-aged proprietress of The Muted Parrot, tucks her pirate wench skirts under her and pulls up a chair after setting a plate of scones on our table. "Who is it? Is it that handsome single dad from your lunch yesterday?"

"I heard Pop's going to play matchmaker for all your kids," I tell her in a desperate bid to distract her.

It doesn't work. "Meh. He says that every couple months like clockwork. Tell me it's the single dad. He's a handsome one. And those muscles—mm-mmm. And so very polite and apologetic after the pizza mishap."

"*The pizza mishap!*" I say triumphantly. "He kissed me on the sidewalk, and then the pizza mishap happened too. *This is not a coincidence.*"

"Ellie thinks she and Wyatt are cursed and should break up," Monica tells Libby.

"Ah. Fear of commitment. Natural, after what happened with the last one she dated."

"Monica's marrying *that last one I dated*'s brother tomorrow," I remind Libby.

"But she's not marrying that barnacle you escaped from, thank goodness. They're brothers, not clones. Now, you explain to me what's bothering you about committing to this nice young man."

"His name's Wyatt," Monica supplies. "The hot single dad. He's in the military and flies experimental planes. Total badass with a big heart."

"Not helping," I tell her.

"You're welcome," she replies, lifting a scone. "Oh, white chocolate raspberry. Libby, you are a goddess."

"Come, come, tell us the problem," Libby says. "Physical, emotional, or vaporal?

"Vaporal?"

"Pits, feet, or ass stinks?"

Monica chokes on her scone.

"He smells very nice," I concede, because despite actually having a good excuse to fake break up with him—since we're only fake dating—I *am* willing to be his friend.

For Beck's sake.

One day, my brother's going to crack the wrong joke and need the rest of us to fall in line to get him out of trouble, and Wyatt and I sniping at each other won't help.

"Does he have performance issues?" Libby asks.

"No matter how I answer that question, it won't be three hours before everyone in town thinks they know everything there is to know about my sex life."

"Two lattes and an ice pack," the barista says, setting coffees and a bag of ice with a dish towel on the table. "And this is why I recommend padded headboards."

"Your face does kinda speak for itself," Libby tells me with a grave nod of her short graying curls.

"I walked into an open cabinet door."

"I threw out my hip trying a new position once. Took me four days to walk again, but the memories last a lifetime. Ah, to be young and nimble again."

"Wyatt's stationed in Georgia, and my job is in Copper Valley, okay?" I need something, or I'll be hearing everyone's opinions on my love life before we make it the two blocks to the town square to try our hand at digging up old Thorny Rock's treasure. "Yes, we have attraction, but we have other things working against us."

"But only until his commitment with the military's up," Monica points out. "Less than two years, right?"

"And he's divorced." I feel like a heel tossing out *that* tidbit, but anything to get them to think he's not perfect. "You know the odds of divorce go up once you've done it the first time." Isn't that what they say?

Libby and Monica share a look. "Cold feet," Libby declares.

"And some history," Monica agrees. "Ellie. I don't hang out with your brother's crowd *ever*, and even I know Wyatt only got married because she was pregnant and he thought it was the right thing to do."

Libby frowns. "Boy didn't know to use a condom?"

"He hooked up with an old girlfriend after his mom's funeral," I whisper, because I feel like I'm cheating on Wyatt by telling other people his business, but I don't want them thinking he goes around having unprotected sex with any woman who'll have him. He used a condom with *me* at Christmas, and we didn't get far enough to need one last night. "I haven't asked, but you know those things break sometimes. Cut him some slack. And Tucker's an awesome kid."

Monica smiles at me over her latte. She's a smiling parrot bride, but she looks like a cat with a canary.

Libby smiles too. "Well then. *Clearly* you're right, and you two aren't meant for each other."

I'm being reverse psychologied. It won't work. "Exactly." I'm oddly deflated, like I *do* actually care that we could have a real chance. Or maybe I'm getting that good at subconsciously acting.

Monica and Libby share another smile, and Libby pushes back from the table. "You two enjoy your coffee. Monica, hon, you let me know if there's anything we can do to help with the wedding. Love your costume, by the way."

"Thanks, Libby."

"You bet."

"Where's Jason?" I ask her when we're alone again at the table.

"Picking out our shovels," she answers cheerfully. "Eat up, Ellie. We're about to dig up gold."

FIFTEEN

Wyatt

DAVIS DECLINES JOINING Tucker and me down in Shipwreck for the kick-off to the treasure dig, so it's just the two of us walking along Blackbeard Avenue, heading for the center square. We haven't yet figured out any of the clues to find the hidden peg leg around town, but neither of us cares. We're having fun with everything else.

"Dad, can I get a tattoo?" Tucker asks.

"What? No. You're seven."

"Motherfucker! Motherfucker!" a voice calls.

I clap my hands over Tucker's ears and look around at the various tourists joining us on the sidewalk, but they're all just as confused as I am.

Grady Rock pops his shaggy head out of the bakery. "Hush your craw, Long Beak Silver. There are kids around."

We all follow his gaze to the cannons sticking over the edge of the roof at Cannon Bowl next door, where old Pop's parrot is perched. "Eat shit," the parrot replies.

"Ah, go walk the plank," Grady says.

The parrot waddles to the end of the cannon, lifts a foot, sways, and plummets toward the ground.

Everyone gasps, but the bird flaps its wings at the last second and takes off across the street to perch on the movie theater's marquee.

"Asshole parrot," Grady mutters as he ducks back into his shop.

I let go of Tucker's ears, but he's stopped and is staring in the bakery window. "*Those* tattoos, Dad," he says.

Oh. Right.

The temporary tattoos that are in baskets all over town. "Oh. Yes."

We grab a handful inside, and Tucker tells Grady he makes the best donuts in the universe, and I end up getting both of us a plain glazed donut for fuel for the dig, though I'm eyeballing the banana pudding donuts. "Banana flavoring?" I ask Grady.

He shudders. "Vanilla pudding with real bananas. They're new. Want one?"

"Ellie will."

That earns me a knowing grin. He glances down at Tucker then back to me, and mouths, *padded headboards*.

I give him a glare that usually makes lieutenants quake, but he just grins bigger.

"Tucker, say thank you for the tattoos," I instruct.

"Aahnk oo," he says around a mouthful of donut.

We make it to the crowded town square just in time to see Pop in full pirate regalia making a speech about the pirate Thorny Rock on the makeshift stage in the center of the square. Tucker tugs my hand, and I follow, thinking we're heading for a better view, or to get closer to what looks to be the line.

But nope.

He's pulling us over to gawk at a group in full costume.

The men are dressed as pirates, but the women are a dog, a monkey, and a parrot.

"Do you think that one uses bad words?" Tucker asks me while he points.

The parrot turns our way, and—oh, *fuck*.

It's Monica.

She waves and gestures us over while the crowd applauds Pop.

"I love your feathers," Tucker tells her, reaching out to pet her stomach.

"Whoa, bud, we ask before we touch," I tell him.

Monica offers an arm instead while I nod to Ellie, who's decked out in the monkey costume. The inside corners of both her eyes are swollen and purply-red, stretching halfway across her lids, and there's no mistaking that she took a hit to the face.

Just like there's no mistaking I took a hit to my right eye, though my bruise is smaller.

She's ridiculously adorable in the costume though.

"That thing hot?" I ask her.

"Not yet, but it will be soon." She casts a glance at the rising sun in the clear blue sky, and I swallow a smile.

"Don't even think about it," she says when I reach for my pocket, like I'm going for my phone to take her picture, but there's an easy smile that she usually doesn't have for me, and seeing the friendliness lifts a weight off my chest I didn't realize I was carrying.

So we *can* be friends.

"Mr. and Mrs. Dixon, have you met Ellie's boyfriend?" Monica asks, turning to an older couple I hadn't realized was with the group, since they're not also in costume. "This is Wyatt and his son, Tucker."

I stifle a wince, because Tucker heard that. Does a seven-year-old understand the difference between *girlfriend* and *girl friend*?

Doesn't matter, I decide. Ellie's my best friend's sister, so odds are, Tucker will see her again. It's okay for him to know grown-ups he can trust, even if he doesn't see them often.

Mr. Dixon—tall, white-haired, and stuffy—barely spares me a glance, but his wife—slender, in pearls and a pantsuit—looks me up and down. A haughty smirk makes her thin face even less attractive. "Dear god, what happened to your face?"

"He accidentally got hit with a log when he was saving a baby from a wolf," Ellie says.

The woman looks at her, and her lip curls as she leaps to the conclusion everyone else apparently has this morning. She turns back to me. "And what do you do?"

"My dad's a superhero," Tucker announces.

"An actor, hm? I suppose that shouldn't surprise me, given the circles Ellie's close to."

"I'm in the Air Force," I correct.

"Oh. A *working* man."

"He has a really cool job testing airplanes," the Blond Caveman's girlfriend says, surprising me.

Surprising the Blond Caveman too, by the looks of the *what the hell?* look he sends her way.

"How do you know what he does?" the caveman asks.

"Ellie told us about it at dinner the other night. Remember?" She smiles at me. "My brother's a commercial pilot. So *thank you*."

"I, ah, work on military jets," I tell her.

"An airplane's an airplane in my world, and I like knowing my brother's safe when he's in the air."

"I like being safe in the air too," Jason announces.

I start to explain that I'm more engineer than pilot, but Ellie jumps in before I can, tugging my arm like the good girlfriend she's playing today. "Guys, don't embarrass him. How much you want to bet Monica finds the most pirate gold?"

"I'm gonna find *all* the pirate gold!" Tucker announces.

"He has a *son*, Ellie?" Mrs. Dixon says with a nose lift.

"No, that's a random kid he kidnapped with candy and donuts yesterday, but he's cute, so we're making him an official pirate with us."

Monica coughs. Her fiancé clears his throat and swipes a hand over his grin. The Blond Caveman glowers. Ellie slips her hand lower until our fingers are intertwined, and fuck me, I could do this all day. "Come on. Are we digging for gold or what?"

"Mom, Dad, you go first," Jason says.

"I can't believe I've lived an hour from here my entire life and never knew I could come here to dig for pirate gold," the Blond Caveman's girlfriend says, falling into line.

"Dad, can we get two shovels?" Tucker asks.

"How about you help me?" Ellie says to him.

"Yeah! I'll dig for you, Miss Captain Ellie. Does your leg hurt today?"

"Not too bad. Thank you for asking."

"Me and Dad got donuts, but we ate them already."

"The banana pudding kind?"

Tucker wrinkles his nose. "No, plain. But Dad said he'd get you one of those pudding ones later. Can I get another donut later too?"

"Absolutely," Ellie says at the same time I say, "One's enough for the day."

Ellie bends down. "I'll sneak you one when he's not looking," she whispers.

Tucker giggles.

And I shake my head at both of them.

"Is she bringing *him* to your wedding, Jason? He's rather… plebian," Mrs. Dixon murmurs loudly in front of us.

"So am I, Mom," Jason replies.

"Honestly, I don't know why you let Monica have a maid of honor who broke your brother's heart. Not that he can't do better, but it's still rude."

"So is talking about people behind their backs, Mrs. Dixon," Ellie says cheerfully.

The Blond Caveman sends Ellie a murderous look.

She smiles back.

"I like you having other enemies besides me," I tell her softly, and she snorts.

"Speaking of," she replies, just as soft, "we can't have sex anymore. It's too dangerous."

That's a challenge if I ever heard one. "We'll discuss this in bed tonight."

"We will *not*," she whispers.

"Bathtub works too."

She gives me the old Ellie Ryder *you're pissing me off* glare, and I don't even try to tuck in a grin at how easy it still is to get her.

She huffs as she obviously realizes what I'm doing.

"Or maybe over strip ping-pong?" she murmurs.

Dammit.

There I go, popping a boner in public with my kid with me again.

She doesn't look down, but she smiles triumphantly like she knows she won this round.

And honestly?

I'll give it to her.

Because I like that smile.

She works hard. She's dressed in a monkey costume in eighty-degree weather to make her best friend happy. And when I went snooping on her social media pages last night, I discovered post after post of shared *help find this pet a home* messages.

The last time she posted a personal picture was before Christmas.

Nothing about her accident.

Nothing about recovery.

The only pictures of her were posted by her parents or her friends.

So seeing her smile?

It's like watching her come back to life.

Beck might've been pulling her leg about me having a problem, but he wasn't lying about Ellie's accident affecting her.

Monica's grinning widely as she hands me a shovel. "Get to work, Wyatt. This gold won't dig itself up. Show me those muscles."

The Blond Caveman yanks a shovel out of the pile and stalks off. "C'mon, Sloane, I'll show you how a real man digs for treasure," he says.

Monica and Ellie share a look. Tucker looks up at both of them, and says, "C'mon, Miss Captain Ellie. I'm gonna be a real man too," and even the Blond Caveman's girlfriend cracks up.

"Dad, I'm going to beat you," Tucker adds.

"Oh, you think so?"

"He's totally going to beat you," Ellie says.

He grins at me behind his glasses, and *fuck*, how am I going to survive having to give him back to Lydia at the end of the summer?

I shove away the panic, because that's a problem for another day.

For now, I have pirate treasure to dig.

With my fake girlfriend.

Who just might be turning out to be more than I ever thought she could be.

Yep. Saving that problem for another day too.

SIXTEEN

Ellie

MY BRAIN IS BROKEN.

It's like the *How we feel about Wyatt* switch got flipped overnight, and now, instead of *annoying as a gnat*, he's at *hot as fuck*.

Or possibly I'm overheating in this monkey costume.

But watching him shovel dirt in the town square is making me horny in ways I can't ever remember being horny.

He hasn't even taken his shirt off, and he's *still* smokin' hot.

"No, Miss Ellie, let me do that for you," Tucker says.

He's skin and bones, but he's putting his all into thrusting the short shovel into the soft earth, shrieking with glee every time he finds a plastic pirate coin.

I should really talk to Pop about getting some biodegradable pirate coins.

Yes.

That.

I should concentrate on how I can help make the Pirate Festival more earth-friendly.

Not on the way Wyatt just wiped his face with his T-shirt, exposing half of his six-pack and making ten women around us drop their shovels, including a pirate wench who just murmured, "I'd tap that."

"He's taken," Monica tells her.

"Lucky woman."

My cheeks burn, but I don't disagree. "I can dig a few shovels," I tell Tucker. "I'm not helpless."

"I'm being shrivelpuss," he informs me.

"Chivalrous," Wyatt corrects with a grin.

"That means helping people because I'm a gentleman," Tucker explains.

"And you're doing a fantastic job," Wyatt agrees. "But if Miss Ellie wants to dig some, you can let her have fun too."

"But she'll get her monkey fur all dirty."

Such a sweet kid. "You're the most chivalrous pirate I've ever met," I tell him.

"Oh! Look! I found a pearl necklace!" Sloane exclaims.

All of the Dixons whip their heads around to look as she pulls a string of Mardi Gras beads from the ground.

"Those are *fake*," Mrs. Dixon sniffs.

Sloane drapes them over her neck. She's not sweating at all in her dog costume, nor does she seem at all the least bit offended that she had to play the dog. "They're a fabulous addition to my collar, aren't they, Patrick?"

He rolls his eyes. "Sure."

"Are we nearly done?" Mrs. Dixon asks Jason.

"No way," he replies. "We could dig for *days* and not find all the treasure they hid here."

His mother goes pale. She takes a step and her heels twist in the dirt. "This is a safety hazard."

"That's why there are signs everywhere to wear boots," Jason tells her.

"Big eyesore the rest of the year, isn't it?" Mr. Dixon says.

"They'll plant flowers in half of it and sod the rest when the week's over," Wyatt tells him.

I shoot him a look.

"I read the festival website," he says. "You hot? Want a break?"

"Oh my god, Ellie, you're so red you're purple. Go sit down," Monica orders.

"I'm fine," I tell her.

It *is* really fucking hot in this costume.

"Wyatt, do you know the most important thing about a wedding?" Monica asks.

"The bride's always right?"

"Correct. Now go make sure Ellie sits down and has something to drink."

Tucker looks wide-eyed between all the adults.

"You can stay with me, because you're a good pirate treasure digger," Monica tells him.

I squint my eyes at her, because is she *trying* to get me to strip for Wyatt?

She doesn't bat a lash of acknowledgment.

"Can I, Dad? Please?"

"We'll be right here," Monica tells him. "And Jason knows CPR, and he always carries a first aid kit."

That's such baloney, and judging by the way Wyatt's lips twist and his eyes narrow, he knows it.

"If she dies of heat stroke, it's on you," Monica tells him. "Are you a good boyfriend or not?"

"All right, all right. C'mon, Ellie. Let's go get you out of this costume and into some air conditioning."

"She loves the banana pudding at Crusty Nut," Monica offers.

"I know," he tells her.

Of course he does.

He fought me over which one of us got to put the bedspread covered in last night's banana pudding into the washing machine this morning.

I let him win, but only because I had a call come in from an employee who needed to take an emergency sick day because her daughter was diagnosed with appendicitis.

And also because I know he didn't forget the deal he offered, whereby he'd get to see my doodle pad.

"I'm not that hot," I tell him when he stops beside me.

"Just dead sexy hot," he replies.

Heat funnels to my core, and I try to stutter out a response, but before I can, he bends and tosses me over his shoulder.

I gasp in surprise.

"That hurt?" he asks quietly.

"No," I answer honestly, half-surprised.

"Good. Tell me if it does. And don't be a stubborn ass." He turns, and adds, "Tucker, I'll be right over there if you need me, okay?"

"Okay, Dad."

He marches across the field, me hanging on with my monkey butt in the air, and while I get the occasional twinge in my leg, it doesn't hurt.

I can't see Tillie Jean's face when Wyatt marches us into the Crusty Nut, but I can hear her. "Table for two?"

"By the window if you can," he tells her.

"How about the balcony, sugar?"

"Is it out of the sun?"

"You bet."

"Sounds great."

"Sorry about my butt, Tillie Jean," I offer.

"Cutest pirate monkey butt we've had come in so far this morning," she replies. "C'mon. I got a table with an umbrella and a great view of the treasure hunt."

"You got clothes on under that?" Wyatt asks while he carries me up the stairs.

I'd argue about this, but I'm tired of arguing with him. "Enough that I can unzip," I confirm.

"Hot dog, it's my lucky day."

I shouldn't be amused, but once again, Wyatt made a joke, and now I'm laughing.

He finally puts me down next to a wrought iron patio table and lets me take my own seat under the umbrella Tillie Jean cranks up for us. After standing at the railing a minute, he waves at Tucker across the street, and then takes his own seat.

"Did Monica just set us up on a date?" I ask him. "I mean, not that she doesn't believe we're dating, but...like on a *real* date. Alone. Is that what this is supposed to be?"

"That depends. Who's paying?"

I toss a sugar packet at him. "Very funny."

He smiles at me, and *hello*, gooey insides. Wyatt Morgan is *not* supposed to turn me all mushy and sappy.

But he's doing an excellent job of it.

I wave a hand at my hot face, then belatedly realize I can unzip my monkey costume. I pull my arms out, and breathe a sigh of relief when the light summer breeze touches my bare skin.

Wyatt swallows a smile and glances at the menu Tillie Jean left.

"Has Beck called you today?" I ask him, because Beck's a safe topic.

Kind of.

He shakes his head.

"Does that make you nervous?" I ask.

He frowns slightly, like he's puzzled, then shakes his head again. "I think he's trying to set us up."

"Look, we can be friends, and it's nice of you to humor me with claiming to be my boyfriend this week, but we seriously *cannot* be anything more."

He leans back in his chair and watches me while our server delivers water glasses and asks if we need another minute.

"Yes," he says at the same time I ask for a basket of gold nuggets—aka fried pickles—and a banana pudding.

"Hush," I say to his raised eyebrows. "Patrick's parents make me nervous, okay?"

"Make it two, please," he tells the server, and she scuttles away with a smile.

Like she, too, thinks we're on a date, and she, too, thinks we're cute.

Not good.

Because even if Wyatt was relationship material, I'm not.

SEVENTEEN

Wyatt

WHEN OUR SERVER LEAVES, Ellie leans into the table. "Why would Beck be trying to set us up?" she half-whispers. She doesn't look annoyed.

More like anxious.

"He's worried about you," I tell her.

"Did you...tell him?" she asks.

She doesn't say *what*, but she doesn't have to. I shake my head. "You?"

"It was none of his fucking business." She huffs. "That didn't come out right."

I start to smile, but she chews on her bottom lip, which simultaneously sends blood flowing straight to my cock and puts my pulse on high alert, because the Ellie I've always known would've rolled her eyes and said she was fine.

"Can I tell you something?" she asks.

"Why me?"

"Because if you tell anyone else, I can deny it because of our history."

That's the Ellie I know, and for the first time in my life, I'm finding her huffiness utterly adorable. "Then absolutely."

"I don't know what I want to do with my life."

"I recommend *not* marrying your ex-boyfriend."

She kicks me under the table, and I feel marginally better about myself for that smart-ass comment just popping off my tongue.

"When I graduated high school, I told myself I'd have a master's degree in five years, a husband in eight, and kids in ten," she tells me, which isn't a surprise in the least. "And that I'd work my ass off to earn every promotion I got with my parents, because I *know* they'll leave me the company one day, but I don't want it just because I'm their daughter. I want to fucking *earn* it. I've been saving up to buy them out five years before they think they want to retire because Beck's right, they're workaholics and they don't realize how old they're getting."

"You should probably not use the word *old* when you approach them." *Fuck*, I'm terrible at this. "I mean—"

She cuts me off with a flutter of her hand. "I have two years to practice. I'll get this."

"Of course you will."

"See? That's the thing. I can tell you what I want *professionally*. But I don't have a clue what I want in my personal life anymore."

"You don't want a family anymore?"

"I don't know if I…if I *can*." The words come out like they're physically painful, and the sudden understanding hits me like a sock to the gut that pushes it into my chest to suffocate my heart.

I never wanted to have kids, and then Tucker happened, and I can't imagine my life without him. We talk every night during the school year—I got him a phone over Lydia's objections, and because he's seven, he doesn't know yet he can push limits—and it's the best part of every day.

Ellie's always wanted kids. *Always.*

Life's not fucking fair.

I swallow hard. "The accident?"

"I haven't been…regular…since. And my doctor…doesn't know yet. She says I need more time to heal, but the best way to find out is to…try. And I don't fucking have anyone to try with, and I'm *not* in any position to do it all by myself, or even ready at this point, and I never wanted to do it by myself anyway. But I just—" She looks away and cuts herself off with a shake of her head.

"Does your family know?"

"Of course not. They've barely gotten over the trauma of the phone call. I'm not putting this on them."

"Ellie. They're your *family*."

"And they can't fix it."

I rub a hand over my face, wincing when I accidentally hit my sore eye, and stifle a sigh. "I don't know what all's going on inside your head right now, but I know your mother, and I know she's always been the best listener, with the best advice, and she might not be able to solve anything, but she can sure as hell make anyone feel better."

"I didn't say I feel *bad* about anything."

"But you don't know what you want out of your personal life," I point out. Helpfully.

"Never mind. Forget I said anything."

"You know your worth as a person is more than just whether you can have kids and walk without a limp."

The edges of her pursed lips go white as she glares over the railing at the park.

"If anyone can beat this," I say, "you can."

She doesn't answer.

"Fuck, Ellie, Beck said the doctors weren't sure you'd ever walk again, and look at you, being a dumbass and pushing your limits and giving them the double bird while you dance on tables."

I get a reluctant grin.

"And scientists have made huge advancements in anatomically correct, realistic looking robots, so there's even a chance you'll be able to at least *look* like you're married before you're fifty," I add.

She spins in her chair and lunges for the ketchup, and before I know what's happening, I'm staring down a squeeze bottle. "That wasn't very nice," she says primly.

Her eyes are dancing behind the bruises, and *dammit*, she's pretty when she smiles.

And when she threatens me with a ketchup bottle.

"You can try it," I tell her, "but I'm a quick draw with the mustard."

Her gaze darts to the yellow squirt bottle on the table, then back to me. "You think so?"

"I could definitely sword fight you with it."

"If you want to get stabbed in the heart with a ketchup spout."

"You'd go for my heart?"

"I'm ruthless, Morgan. *Ruthless.*"

"But have you studied the art of war?"

"I've studied the art of not getting trampled by my dear brother, which is the same thing."

"Is not."

"Oh, please. It is—hey!"

I snag the mustard bottle and point it at her while she's distracted with arguing.

"I should squirt you," she says, but she's smiling so big she can't get it out without a laugh.

"Wouldn't be the first time."

"Oh, like yesterday was *my* fault?"

I want to kiss her.

I want to lean across this table and kiss her until neither one of us can breathe, and then I want to kiss her more.

Because she's strong. *So* fucking strong. She's what I *want* to be. What I try to be.

Unstoppable. Undaunted by a challenge. Fearless.

"All your fault," I say. "You set me up."

She's leaning in like she feels it too. Like she would kiss me too.

She's still pointing the ketchup bottle at me, but it's Ellie, so naturally.

"You are so full of baloney."

She's a Siren, beckoning me with her wide smile and daring insults. She's bold and driven and *fun*.

Fuck, I miss fun.

"You like baloney," I remind her.

She wrinkles her nose.

"You did. When we were kids."

The ketchup bottle wavers. "How do you even remember that?"

"It was horrifying."

"You used to eat canned meat. You can't talk."

We're so close, the nozzles on our condiment bottles are touching. "And how do you remember that?"

"My mother tells the story every time your name comes up. *That poor Wyatt Morgan, we had to introduce him to real lunch meat. Think what would've happened to the boy's diet if he'd never moved in down the street.*"

"Lies. All lies." So very close. I could kiss her. I shouldn't, but I could.

Her gaze dips to my lips, a smile growing, and I'm nearly there when she suddenly jerks back and squirts ketchup across my shirt.

She gapes for a minute at me, suspended in shock. "Oh, shit," she gasps. "I didn't mean—"

I squeeze my bottle and get her with mustard across her chin and neck.

She squirts again, and I dive out of my chair to miss the red stream. *"That was an accident, you jerk!"* she shrieks.

"Likely story," I retort, aiming the mustard just to her right.

A bird squawks indignantly. "Motherfucker, kiss my ass." There's a flap of wings, and Long Beak Silver shoots into the air with a streak of yellow that wasn't on his feathers before.

We both stare at the bird.

"Oh my god, you shot Long Beak Silver," Ellie whispers in horror.

"All your fault," I repeat, hastily stealing her ketchup bottle and moving all the condiments two tables away.

She's wiping the mustard off her face when Davis appears at the top of the stairs. His man bun is freshly straightened, his beard thick enough to be hiding a squeeze bottle, and he's shaking his head. "Foreplay?"

"Shut up," Ellie says.

I grab a napkin and wipe the mustard she missed under her jaw.

"How's the patient?" I ask him.

"Sitting pretty with Ellie at 802,700, but I could change that to my name."

"You are a god," Ellie tells him. "I could even kiss that flea-infested beard. Sit. Lunch is on Wyatt."

"So generous," Davis replies. "Where's your kid?"

I point to the treasure dig. "With the human parrot."

"Ah. Anyway, bill's in the mail. I'm heading home."

"But you just got here," Ellie says while I add, "Kick up your feet and stay a while."

"No can do. I've got a reactor to hack." He turns his gaze to Ellie. "We're even now. Don't break it again."

"Swear on the penalty of having to watch Beck do a photo shoot, I will not touch Frogger again for the rest of my life."

"Kiss her for me," he adds to me. He gives us both a salute and disappears down the stairs again.

"You are *not* kissing me," Ellie whispers.

"Now it's a challenge," I tell her.

"I'm so freaking serious, Wyatt. We can be friends, but we *cannot* touch, kiss, get naked, take baths, or do any other thing that people who date do. We will literally die. The universe does *not* want us together."

And on top of that, she has a life in Copper Valley, and my situation is complicated.

"We have to touch at the very least," I point out, because I'm apparently a masochistic idiot. "I'm your boyfriend this week. Your wedding date. Remember?"

"Fine. Touching. But only in public, and only when *absolutely* necessary. And we should probably both wear protective gear to bed—which we're going to *separately*—and take shifts sleeping in case the house burns down around us."

I don't bother trying to hide my grin. "Sure. We'll set up a schedule."

"Don't mock me. I'm serious."

"As a heart attack?" I prompt.

She swats at my hand. "*Do not tempt fate,*" she hisses.

"All right, all right. No touching, no kissing, no nothing unless absolutely necessary to sell your story."

"Thank you."

She smiles.

I smile.

Boundaries should be a good thing. I don't have room in my life for falling for Ellie Ryder. Not with the added complications it would bring.

But agreeing to her new terms feels more fake than pretending to be her boyfriend for the wedding.

And I don't want to think about what *that* means.

EIGHTEEN

Ellie

BECAUSE A WEDDING at the Pirate Festival is a big deal—especially since Shipwreck is competing with the Unicorn Festival in the small town of Sarcasm not ten miles away—Monica and Jason are guest judges for the pirate costume, ship model, and food contests, and the entire wedding party is invited along to help offer opinions. So Wednesday night, Wyatt, Tucker, and I join Monica, Jason, and their families at the Deep Blue Retreat Center, where dozens of pirate ship models are on display in the semi-circular conference room, which has windows overlooking the soft, hazy mountain ridges on either side of Shipwreck.

"These are amazing," Monica says as we walk along the curved row of tables holding the ships submitted by the school-age kids in Shipwreck. Some are made of Legos, some out of popsicle sticks, some out of clay, but they're all adorable and really cool in which details the kids picked to highlight.

Almost all of them have a fake bird, and at least half have signs added about no cussing on deck.

My personal favorite is the one made out of recycled food containers, and I know Monica's totally going to vote for that one too, since her day job is making art out of recycled materials.

"Dad, can I make a pirate ship?" Tucker asks.

"Sure. I've got some Legos for you at home."

"No, Dad, to enter in the contest!"

"Next year, bud. They're closed this year."

"I'll judge your ship, Tucker," Monica tells him. "And I'd bet it'll be awesome."

They're best friends since hanging out digging for treasure this morning.

"How's your leg today?" Monica's mom asks me as we make our way to the next room, which has tables and tables loaded down with pirate-themed food.

"Better than a peg leg," I tell her.

"Dad! Dad, can I have an octopus?" Tucker asks.

Wyatt catches him by the shoulders. "Slow down, there, Captain Hollow Leg. See Miss Monica's scoring chart? She needs to decide what's pretty before we taste it, and then she has to rate how good it is."

"No need to worry, we have extras for the wee ones." Pop Rock ambles over, dressed today like his ancestor, Thorny Rock. "Right this way, right this way."

My stomach gives a timely growl, and Monica laughs. "Go on, Ellie. All of you. We'll be done soon."

"I've never eaten a hot dog in my life," Mrs. Dixon murmurs to her husband. "This is the most undignified festival I've ever seen."

"I think it's fun," Sloane declares. "They say fun cures constipation."

Patrick shoots her a look. She smiles back tightly.

And Wyatt and I share a look.

So there's trouble in Patrick-Sloane land.

Pop opens the door to the center's industrial kitchen, and oh my word, the food.

So much food.

Plates and platters of entrées, appetizers, sides, and— "Cookies!" Tucker exclaims.

It's the same food out on display—deviled egg ships with pirate flags, island pizza, quicksand dip, pirate eyeballs, hot dogs cut into wedges with the bottom half sliced to give it octopus legs, meat cannonballs—except there are paper pirate plates and napkins and a huge bowl of pirate punch that's obviously been dipped into.

"Eat up, me hearties," Pop says. "That there be kiddie punch, because me blasted crew drank up all the rum last night."

"Are these meatballs made with chicken?" Mrs. Dixon demands, pointing to the pirate eyeballs.

Monica's mom smiles. She's dressed like a hippie pirate, with a scabbard tied over her flowery muumuu and a pirate hat on her short graying hair. "Yes, Caroline, they're chicken. I called ahead and checked because I knew you'd prefer it."

Wyatt and I both turn around before Mrs. Dixon looks at either of us. He dives for a plate to help Tucker make a few healthy choices before getting to dessert, and I take a minute to wipe the smile off my face as I pretend to decide between the quicksand dip and shovels—aka hummus and vegetables—and the grilled parrot—aka chicken wings.

Ultimately, both win.

We all load up our plates and carry them into the center's dining room, where other judges are eating and discussing the festival. Monica's mom takes the seat beside me at the rectangular table, and Wyatt and Tucker pile in across from us.

Jason's family sits at the table behind me, and I breathe a sigh of relief that I can make any face I want without fear of getting an earful of loudly murmured insults.

"Ellie, honey, how's work?" Monica's mom asks.

I tell her about a few of the projects I've been overseeing. My parents' environmental firm has contracts to retrofit several aging buildings around Copper Valley to improve energy efficiency. We're also working on initiatives with the local government to promote more recycling options around the city, and we've been branching farther and farther into other parts of Virginia, West Virginia, North Carolina, Kentucky, and Tennessee.

She asks Wyatt about his job, and he downplays the whole *flies jets with untested systems* thing, because god forbid the man toot his own horn. Tucker's too busy chowing down on everything on his plate to talk. He has a smear of ketchup across his face, which makes me smile, both because Tucker gets cuter every day, and also because it makes me remember holding Wyatt at ketchup-point this morning.

But then I'm frowning, because I'm not supposed to let myself find Wyatt attractive, since it's bad for our health.

And I probably shouldn't get attached to his son either.

Monica's mom asks how we met and started dating, and we trip over each other telling contradictory stories that all make Tucker giggle, but we're saved by Monica dropping into the seat on the other side of her mother.

"Don't listen to them," Monica says. "Their relationship thrives on one-upping each other. The *real* story is that they've been in love since they were teenagers but were both too stubborn and scared to do anything about it until recently."

I open my mouth to argue, but I realize she's boxed us into a corner.

She grins at me.

And Wyatt leaps up, uses his chair as a vault to fly across the cafeteria table.

"Wha—" I start, turning to watch him leap across the table behind us too. "Oh, shit."

"Oh my god," Monica gasps.

Jason drops his plate upside down and rushes to the table too, where Wyatt's lifting Caroline Dixon off her chair and giving her the Heimlich.

Her eyes are huge, her face mottling, lips parted and bluing at the edges as she struggles to breathe.

Wyatt thrusts his fist under her breastbone once, twice, and on the third thrust, a piece of meatball flies out of her mouth and lands square on Patrick's plate. I don't know where Sloane or Mr. Dixon are, but they're not at the table.

It's just Mrs. Dixon and Patrick, who's now rushing toward his mother too.

She gasps and sags and makes a very unladylike expression that's too garbled to fully be called an expletive, but I'm pretty sure she just said *fuck*.

Wyatt helps her to sitting. "Okay now?" he asks.

She gulps hard, panting, and nods without looking at him.

"Back up, give her space," Patrick snaps. He shoves Wyatt out of the way and squats. "Are you okay? Is anything broken? Did he crack a rib?"

"He saved her life, you jackass," Jason snaps, approaching quickly from the other side of the long table.

"Quit fighting," she rasps out. "And hand me a drink."

Adrenaline belatedly makes my veins fizz. My legs wobble while Wyatt quietly steps away from the Dixons and returns the long way to our table.

"My dad's a hero," Tucker whispers.

"You're damn right," Monica says softly, her voice thick too.

Her mother's fanning her face, eyes bright like she's fighting back tears. "Lordy goodness," she murmurs. "That was scary as all dickens."

Tucker's eyes are huge, borderline scared, and I reach across the table to squeeze his little hand. "Hey. It's okay."

"Did she die?"

"No, sweetie. She's okay."

He glances at his plate, full of hot dog octopi and big chunks of fruit and cookies. Then back at all the grown-ups fussing and panicking belatedly at the next table.

"Just chew it good," I tell him.

He nods and gives me a brave smile, and I suddenly don't know how I could do it.

How do you protect someone you love so much from ever getting hurt? Or let them hurt when they have to?

How do you survive it?

My respect for Wyatt is growing by the second.

Parenthood isn't for the weak.

Monica heads to help Jason, and her mom sinks back to her seat, but I watch Wyatt casually walk past two families at the end of the rows of tables, all gaping at him like he's the hero Tucker knows him to be, while he keeps his head down, hands in his pockets.

He doesn't look up until he's back in his seat next to Tucker, and then, his focus is all on his son. "Ah-ah, I saw that. Fruit swords before treasure cookies."

Tucker grins, his fear fading with Wyatt beside him again. "Good job, Dad."

I could probably explain what I do next, but I don't want to.

Let's just say it ends with me bending across the table, grabbing Wyatt by the cheeks, and planting a kiss worthy of a hero on his lips.

And there might've been some belated applause.

For him being a hero, I mean.

Not for me kissing him.

Because that would be ridiculous.

And dangerous.

But two hours later, I'm grateful to be safe and sound back in Beck's house. No deer or foxes or wolves darted in front of my car, and clearly they didn't get Wyatt either, since he pulls up right behind me.

Neither of us has said another word about Mrs. Dixon choking.

Or about me kissing the stuffing out of him.

And I'm not planning on mentioning it.

Especially the kissing part.

Until I walk through the basement door from the garage and realize there's a huge water stain over the bar. "What—" I start, and then I know.

"The dishwasher," Wyatt and I say in unison.

"I started it before we left." He scrubs a hand over his face. "Davis probably didn't notice."

I just gape at him and continue to point at the ceiling.

"I know, I know," he sighs. "I'll go get towels."

I should argue that I'll clean it up. That this is my fault for kissing him. But I know he'll insist on helping, and then we'll be within *looking* distance of each other, and I'm really, really starting to be convinced that we probably shouldn't ever even live in the same town. "I'm going to bed. And I'm locking the door," I inform him.

He smirks. "You're ridiculous."

"Dad, can I watch baseball?" Tucker asks through a yawn.

I don't wait to hear his answer, because I'm already starting to get attached to *both* of them.

The universe is being a real dick.

Or maybe I need to quit looking for what's *easy*—like Wyatt just landing in my lap this week—and actually figure out what I want to do about getting my life back on track.

He was right this morning.

The doctors *didn't* know if they'd be able to repair my hip and leg enough for me to ever walk again.

But here I am. Limping my stiff self up the stairs.

I *am* going to be physically fine again.

It's time to figure out what the rest of me needs.

NINETEEN

Wyatt

THE THINGS I do for my friends.

When Beck asked me to irritate Ellie, I had a vague idea what I was in for. A prickly porcupine sniping at me? Yep, because I knew just how to poke it. Glares hot enough to melt iron? Wouldn't have her any other way.

That uncomfortable feeling in my dick every time I thought of her naked?

Can't say I haven't been dealing with that anyway these past six months, when I wasn't letting the guilt seep in.

Getting my toes done with Tucker, Ellie, Monica, Jason, the Blond Caveman, Sloane, and the mothers of the happy couple? At the Yo Ho Ho Spa?

Didn't even cross my mind.

But here I am, in a fancy-ass massage chair with one foot soaking in a tub of flowery-scented water while a woman I've never met buffs, slathers, rubs, and does all kinds of weird shit to the other.

Tucker erupts in giggles every time his pedicurist tries to touch his feet, so she's given up and is letting him suck on a pirate lollipop and just soak his toes in the bubbly spa water.

"Smile, honey," Ellie says from her seat on the other side, holding up her phone to get a selfie of the three of us.

I glare at her.

She smiles bigger.

Tucker laughs.

"Beck gets this done all the time," she tells me.

"He also parades around in his skivvies. Are you texting this to him? I will…" I wiggle my brows at her, a clear threat to kiss her, or touch her, or cause some other disaster to befall us "…if you text that picture to *anyone*. Or post it on social media. Or do anything other than delete it."

Her brows twitch like her face is battling between scowling at me and giving me the *I dare you* look.

"It takes a man very secure in his masculinity to get his toes done," Monica calls to me from her seat in a massage chair on the opposite wall.

The Blond Caveman has his nose tucked inside a financial magazine and ignores her.

Jason grins at me. "She's right, you know."

"Oh, hush. Wyatt has no issues with his masculinity," Ellie says. "You should've seen him mopping the floor of the kitchen last night."

"*You* should've seen *us* mopping the floor," I tell her.

"I was a big helper," Tucker says proudly. "I mopped *buckets* full."

Monica sends a quizzical glance at Ellie.

"Dishwasher flooded," Ellie explains.

"Well, thank god it was Beck's house," Monica says.

I choke on a laugh, because that, at least, is the truth. I texted him a picture and told him Ellie and I got carried away doing the dishes.

He replied with a picture of his middle finger, and his assistant pinged me two minutes later to say that she'd scheduled a drywaller to come in and repair the water damage next week, and to enjoy washing dishes by hand in the meantime since the earliest she could get a new dishwasher was five to seven days.

This morning, I woke up to a message from him that he

couldn't ask for a better boyfriend for his sister, except maybe Levi, because his ass is nicer than mine.

I haven't told Ellie, because we'll sort that all out after the wedding's over, when she doesn't need me to play this role anymore.

Fuck, I hope I don't lose a friend over this.

But if I do, I probably didn't deserve him as long as I had him anyway.

"Want me to paint pirate flags on your toes?" my foot lady asks.

Ellie dissolves in a fit of laughter.

"You don't have to get nail polish," Monica tells me with a grin.

"Yeah," I tell the lady. "Pirate flags."

Ellie laughs so hard she has a coughing fit that ends with her gasping and rubbing her leg, but she's still smiling, so there's that. Her foot lady has to stop. Jason gives me a thumbs up. The Blond Caveman rolls his eyes behind his magazine, which he's not using very effectively to block his face.

When we're done, I have pirate flags on my two big toes, and I look like an idiot, but I don't really care. Tucker thinks it's awesome and begs me to take a picture to send to his mom.

I oblige while I'm waiting to pay, and when I get to the front, the cashier smiles. "Mother of the groom took care of you, your son, and your girlfriend. Go show off those pretty toes, and come back and see us again!"

Outside, Mrs. Dixon is speed-walking toward the hotel at the end of the street. Jason and Monica and her mom are talking to Ellie and Sloane while the Blond Caveman makes a phone call.

I stop next to Jason. "Your mom didn't have to pay for us."

"It's the only way she'll say thank you." He claps me on the shoulder. "Don't mention it or she'll get bitchy again. We're heading to the food trucks on the square. You guys coming?"

"Wyatt promised Tucker another trip to the water park," Ellie answers for us. "They'll catch up with us later."

"You want to go with them?" Monica asks. "We're just going to be walking and stuffing our faces and badgering Patrick into wearing a pirate hat and an eye patch. You'll have more fun at the water park."

"I didn't bring my swimsuit."

"I have six."

"Monica."

"Oh, hush. Don't give me that *I'm here for the bride* stuff. When's the last time you went down a water slide?"

"I can't—"

"And the lazy river? You *love* the lazy river."

"Babe, *you* love the lazy river," Jason says. "Let's all go."

"Yeah!" Tucker cheers.

Ellie tries to send Monica another meaningful look, but it's completely lost on the bride.

"Nobody cares about your scar," I tell her quietly.

"*I* care," she mutters.

I study her a minute.

She's not meeting my gaze, and her cheeks are going pink.

She's soaked in the tub at least three nights this week, so I know the water itself isn't the issue.

It's the swimsuit.

"Give me thirty minutes," I tell her.

Her brows furrow. "For what?"

"A solution. C'mon, Tucker. We've got a job to do."

"You're not bailing on us, are you?" Monica asks.

"Nope. Meet you there. Make sure Ellie's with you."

I don't know if my idea's even possible, but it's worth a try. And if there's anywhere that can pull it off, it's Shipwreck.

TWENTY

Ellie

I AM in severe like with Wyatt Morgan.

The man found me scuba shorts.

He activated Shipwreck's gossip network and found me scuba shorts that cover me down to the knee, completely hiding my scars.

We spend the entire afternoon at the water park, destroying our pedicures, Jason and Wyatt trying to out-cannonball each other, floating around on the lazy river, helping Tucker learn to swim, laughing as he climbs through the two-story pirate adventure sky fort with its water cannons and dodges the water that dumps out of the giant bucket on top, and soaking up the gorgeous afternoon sunshine.

I bypass the water slides, but Tucker and Wyatt go down them a million times.

Monica declares it naptime around five and gives me a gentle push toward Wyatt's car. "Go home. Jason and I are having a pizza-in-the-room night and leaving the families to fend for themselves. We'll see you for the rehearsal in the morning, okay?"

"Not The Grog?" We missed it last night with all the worry over Mrs. Dixon almost choking.

"Oh my god, Ellie, I am so tired," she says with a laugh. "Besides, I think Jason's feeling neglected."

"If you need anything—"

"My mom's here. And you know all I have to do is lift a finger and any of the Rock family will be right on it."

"C'mon, Ellie," Wyatt says. He waves at somebody on a bike, and the rider slows as he approaches, a double-handled plastic bag dangling from the handlebars. "Train's leaving in three minutes."

"Mr. Morgan?" the kid on the bike says.

"Yep." Wyatt hands him a couple twenties, and the kid hands over the bag.

"Is that fried chicken?" I ask, sniffing the air.

"And potato salad, french fries, banana pudding, and a funnel cake. Ordered it all from the food trucks."

"Jason, I'm sorry, I'm marrying Wyatt tomorrow instead," Monica announces.

"Shut your mouth, he's mine," I retort without thinking.

She grins at me, and I feel my cheeks heat up.

And not because of all the sun this afternoon.

"Girls are weird," Tucker announces. "I'm never getting married. Except maybe to my sister if I ever have one. Can I have a sister?"

For once, Wyatt seems to be speechless.

"You should ask Santa for a sister," I tell Tucker while I herd him into Wyatt's SUV. "Sisters are the best. I know, because I am one."

"Sisters are annoying," Wyatt corrects.

"He's just jealous because he never had one," I whisper to Tucker, who giggles while he pulls his seat belt over his booster seat. "Sisters are totally awesome."

Tucker loops his arms around my neck and hugs me tight, and surprised, I hug him back.

"You're awesome, Miss Captain Ellie."

"Not as awesome as you."

We make it back to Beck's house without incident and dive

into the food like we haven't eaten in a week. Tucker tries two bites of banana pudding and declares it gross.

"Then I guess it's my paternal duty to eat yours," Wyatt announces.

"Hello, we *share* it," I argue.

"He's not your kid."

"Tucker, may I please have half of your banana pudding?"

He looks between us. "It's nice to share, Dad," he finally whispers.

"It really is, Dad," I agree.

"Bath time for you," Wyatt tells him without answering either of us.

But he leaves half a carton of banana pudding in the fridge when he takes Tucker upstairs.

I clean up the dinner mess, realizing with a start that it's been days since I cleaned up in here, yet everything's nearly spotless anyway. Except for our small dinner mess, of course.

Because Wyatt takes care of things.

I've sometimes wondered why Beck stayed close with him. Once the guys started their boy band adventure, an entire new world opened up. Beck, Levi, Tripp, Cash, and Davis could've gone anywhere, done anything. They each lost a few friends along the way—money changes things—but Wyatt was the one constant outside immediate family.

And I think I get it now.

Just like we called Davis to fix Frogger, any one of the guys from the neighborhood could call Wyatt, and he'd have their backs. He'd do anything they needed done.

Including keeping an eye on a sister they're worried about.

Once the dishes are put away, I fix myself a cup of tea—a new habit since the accident—snag my doodle pad from the bedroom and carry it out to the living room. Tucker's crying upstairs. Wyatt's talking to him softly, steady, calm, his deep voice reassuring me too even though I don't realize I need reassurance, nor do I have any idea what he's saying.

It's just the calming cadence of his voice.

Nothing could be that calm and soothing if there was actually a problem. Poor kid's probably exhausted from too much fun.

I glance at email on my phone, decide there's nothing that can't wait until next week, and toss it aside to open my doodle pad instead.

I doodled all the time when I was a kid, but sports, clubs, and other extra-curriculars didn't leave me much time for it in high school or college. It wasn't until I was forced to take two months off work for recovery this winter that I picked it up again.

And it turns out, I realize as I flip through the pages, I had a lot of anger to work through this year.

Dick and the Nuts was supposed to be fun, about a schlong and a pair of peanuts—no, not testicles, actual peanuts, like the legumes—who set out to take over the world despite one of the nuts being on crutches.

Dick was supposed to be a funny, lighthearted evil genius.

He's actually everything I hated about Patrick by the time he broke up with me. Addicted to his job first, his phone second, his bloodline third, and everything else was just gravy. I met Patrick at a fundraiser for Jason's company—clean water and green energy pretty much go hand-in-hand, and my parents like to send corporate dollars from Ryder Consulting toward various nonprofits every year—and I thought we shared a lot of the same passions in life.

I don't know if I looked at him through rose-colored glasses that first year, or if he slowly changed away from the man I thought he was when we met, but by the time this past Christmas rolled around, I was more angry that he'd kept me from meeting my goal of being married and pregnant than that he hadn't proposed.

I should've realized that meant I wanted the wrong thing out of our relationship, but it took a car accident and, honestly, this week for me to fully connect the dots.

There's more to life than marking off checkboxes.

I'm smiling to myself over the Nuts—I named them Joe and Bob, because I'm creative like that—and their plan to put Dick in a trance so they can run the controls on the spaceship to blast the earth with a laser beam that'll give everyone the giggles so they can rob all the chocolate shops they want without anyone raising an alarm, when Wyatt steps down the stairs.

He disappears into the basement, and when he returns with an armful of sheets and the comforter for Beck's bed, I start to get up.

"Move one muscle, and I'm calling Beck and telling him we're getting married."

"That would show the Dixons," I reply. "And you know that's the fastest way to get Beck here. He loves weddings. And me. And sometimes you."

Wyatt grins.

I grin back.

He's not winning this round.

"I'll swap out your bubble bath for itch powder," he offers.

"You would not."

"Wanna bet?"

"You don't *have* itch powder."

"Last time I stayed here, your brother salted my sheets and put a life-size taxidermied bear in my bedroom to scare the shit out of me. I owe him. So yeah, I brought itch powder."

And I'm suddenly quite certain I don't want the man making the bed I'm going to sleep in tonight.

I start to move again. "*Sit*," he orders.

Damn, that military order voice is hot.

Hot hot.

And that's why I sit.

Because if I follow Wyatt into the bedroom, the mattress won't be the only thing undressed.

"Thank you," I say, conceding with a regal nod. "Also, if you itch powder my sheets, I'll itch powder your underwear."

He just grins again.

Which is also freaking hot.

I go back to flipping through my doodles. After a few minutes, Wyatt appears again. He stops in the kitchen before joining me with a water bottle in one hand and the rest of the banana pudding in the other. He claims the recliner angled to give him a view of both me and the scenery of the town below—or it would, if dusk wasn't falling—and props up the footrest. "Trade you," he says, lifting the banana pudding and pointing to my doodle pad.

I hesitate only a moment before I lean over, ignoring the twinge in my hip and thigh, to snatch the pudding and toss him the notebook.

"I was kidding, Ellie." He holds out my book for me to take it back, but I shrug.

"I was going to show you anyway."

"Why?"

"To scare you into your senses so you'll quit trying to kiss me."

He smirks and settles deeper into the recliner as he flips the cover open. "Do I want to know where you got the inspiration for Dick?"

"You don't recognize him?"

Dick's a short, squat, not very pretty penis. He looks nothing like Wyatt's package.

"Can't say I do," he replies easily, completely bypassing the opportunity to ask if I've gotten an eyeful of my brother without the sock the photographers make him put in his briefs.

It's an old joke. Possibly we've worn it out.

Also, possibly I don't want to think about my brother in his underwear. It's been nice having the cardboard cutout of him in the corner turned around.

Wyatt's perceptive gray eyes skim the page, and he snickers.

"Not a word on my talent," I warn him around a mouthful of heaven. I mean, banana pudding. My mom makes awesome banana pudding, but there's something about the meringue on Crusty Nut's banana pudding that puts it head and shoulders above.

"I was laughing at the Nuts," he tells me.

"Oh. Then maybe you do have good taste after all."

Sparring with him is so easy. We've done it a million times. It's habit. But it's also comfortable, which isn't something I ever noticed before.

Maybe it's never been comfortable before.

Or maybe we've both grown up.

Considering how long we've each been legal adults, it's probably past time.

"Why'd you date the Blond Caveman so long?" he asks as he flips another page.

"Ambition made me blind. Why didn't you quit the military?"

His smile fades into a resigned scowl. "Paperwork and networking failure."

"Networking?"

"Need a job to pay child support. Don't have enough experience yet in flight test to be valuable to anyone who'd hire me in Copper Valley. And my request for a waiver to get out of my service commitment got lost on some colonel's desk. Found it last week, got denied."

"Beck always said you'd be career military. That it suits you."

"Shit happens. Rather have Tucker than a long career though." He skims the next page and cackles.

Wyatt Morgan.

Cackling.

Because he thinks my doodles are funny.

My nipples go tight and a familiar heat pools between my legs.

"Broccolisauruses? Eating underwear models?"

"Beck might've pissed me off that day."

"What'd he do, tell you that you couldn't do something?"

"He asked me to be his date to some gala in Paris."

He glances at me in surprise. "That pissed you off?"

"You want to know the last time Beck asked me to be his date to *anything*?"

"Ah."

I think he's done, that he gets it, but instead, he shuts the book and looks at me. "Ever consider he finally realized what he almost lost?"

I open my mouth, but I suddenly don't know if he's talking about Beck, and the possibility of losing a sister, or himself, and the possibility that he might've lost an opportunity.

With me.

Which is crazy, because I have *always* irritated the *shit* out of him.

I used to run marathons. I knew I was pretty—I'm Beck

Ryder's sister, for god's sake, last year's *People*'s Sexiest Man Alive, and we're *clearly* related—and athletic and smart. I didn't have insecurity issues, and so when Wyatt was willing to do the naked tango with me, I assumed it was because he wanted the same thing I did.

A little human companionship and confirmation that I was still attractive to *somebody*.

And possibly he was a little tipsy.

And angry. And hurt. And lonely.

Just like I was, except I wasn't tipsy.

And maybe, just maybe, seeing him lonely and hurt and angry, made me realize what *I'd* been missing all those years between hating him, then crushing on him, then hating him.

That I wouldn't have given him a second thought if there wasn't something *there*.

"I considered a lot of things after the accident," I tell him. "But it's complicated. I don't want pity dates. But I don't want to take anything for granted either, so I understand other people not wanting to take people for granted. But I also wanted everything to go back the way it was before. Except it can't."

"Embrace what's better, Ellie. Change what you can change. Fix what you can fix. Accept the rest."

"You mean like accepting that the house will burn down if we sleep together again?" I whisper.

He gives an exasperated laugh. "Sure."

"Okay. Good. Glad we agree on that."

"You gonna eat that?" he asks with a nod to my banana pudding.

Our banana pudding.

I lean over and hand it to him.

"Did you spit in it?" he asks suspiciously.

And I laugh.

Because we're a little messed up, but for the first time in my life, I'm really glad to have Wyatt as a friend.

TWENTY-ONE

Wyatt

AFTER A LONG AND RESTLESS NIGHT, Tucker and I agree he needs to learn to play air hockey more than he needs to go dig for more pirate treasure or hunt for the peg leg that apparently still hasn't been found in town. Ellie was up early to take the box of parrots into town and get ready for the wedding, but she hung around long enough to have breakfast with us and draw Tucker a parrot for him to color later.

We're scrambling away for the puck mid-morning when I hear the door open and someone hit the security keypad.

"Stay here, bud," I tell Tucker.

I creep softly up the stairs, half expecting to see Beck, and instead, I get a glimpse of an older couple.

My eyes sting and my chest swells, because these two people are the closest thing I have to parents in the entire world.

"Morning," I say.

Mrs. Ryder turns, her bright blue eyes land on me, and her face lights up in a familiar smile that her children share. "Wyatt! We thought you'd be down in Shipwreck with Ellie."

She smothers me in a hug, which is impressive, considering I have over half a foot and at least thirty pounds on her. Mr. Ryder squeezes my shoulder. "Hanging in there?" he asks.

"Always. You, sir?"

"Can't complain."

"Where's that little boy of yours?" Mrs. Ryder demands. "I have presents."

"You didn't have to—"

"Hush. This is what grandmas do."

I know a thing or two about arguing with the Ryders—all of them—and I know it's usually pointless.

Sometimes fun, but always pointless. "Yes, ma'am."

I help Mr. Ryder with the luggage while Mrs. Ryder heads downstairs to hug Tucker. After they're settled, Tucker talks them into heading to town with us for pizza.

Doesn't take much. Just him looking at Mrs. Ryder and asking if she's hungry for pizza too.

Tucker chews her ear off about the pirate festival on the drive down the mountain. I smile as I listen to them chattering back and forth, but worry's creeping in.

Tomorrow, we leave to drive home to Georgia. Monday, I go back to work. He starts at a summer camp that my boss swears his wife loves for their kids.

And we won't have Ellie with us.

For the majority of my life, that was just fine with me. She was irritating, obnoxious, and a general pain in the ass.

Now?

Either I need to see my doctor for an issue with sudden flaming indigestion, or I'm going to fucking miss her.

Because maybe the problem was never that she was irritating, obnoxious, and a general pain in the ass.

Maybe the problem was that she was everything I wanted to be, and then everything I wanted, and nothing I thought I could have, or deserved to have.

Working hard to make something of myself in a career and being the best father I know how to be isn't always enough to erase the seeds planted in my subconscious in my early childhood that I was nothing but a pest.

"Work going well?" Mr. Ryder asks.

I tell him about my current project, an upgrade to radar sensors on the newest fighter platform, and he tells me about a windmill farm project their company's been doing for a cloud-based server complex south of the city, closer to where Davis lives.

"Still looking to get out in a year?" he asks me.

"I'm ready." I'd stay in until retirement if I could—I like knowing my job supports my country and ultimately helps protect my friends and neighbors, and the work is challenging and rewarding—but the odds of being able to get stationed and stay stationed at the base just north of Copper Valley, and therefore close to Tucker, are slim. "Just waiting for the clock to tick down or a waiver to come through."

"You want a job, you know where to find us."

"Appreciate that, sir."

Not that I plan on taking him up on any offer without knowing I've earned it. It was hard enough letting them pay for me to take my SATs so I could apply to college.

Which is exactly the sort of thing that family does, and one more reason I need to not fuck around with Ellie.

Her family means too much to me.

Hell, they're why I applied for an ROTC scholarship the minute I hit campus.

So they wouldn't feel like they needed to help me through.

That was before Beck and the guys hit it big with Bro Code, and before Ellie landed herself a full ride.

And if I fuck things up with her, I'll never again hear the chatter in the back of the car with the way they've adopted Tucker as a surrogate grandkid. I won't feel like I still deserve to be treated like one of their own.

If Ellie and I were both in this for the long haul, that would be one thing.

But she doesn't even want to touch me for fear the world will crumple around her.

So I'll keep my feelings to myself, and Tucker will keep his second set of grandparents, and life will go on, just as it always has.

Except different.

We park once again in the field at the far end of Shipwreck and head down Blackbeard Avenue into town. Mr. Ryder scans the street. "Where do you suppose Ellie is?"

Spotting the bridal party isn't easy this morning—no bright parrot costumes for the wedding day, apparently—but then I notice the English colonists.

And the woman who looks like Kiera Knightly in that pirate movie.

"Ah, there, I'd guess," I tell Mr. Ryder. I don't see Ellie, but Monica, Jason, Sloane, and the parents are in full colonial regalia. It appears Pop Rock is spending the day playing the role of a governor with the powdered white wig.

This town.

I wave to Monica down the block when she glances our way, and her face lights up as she waves back.

"Oh my heavens," Mrs. Ryder murmurs with a smile. "I can only imagine what her bridal gown will look like."

We meet up with them two shops down from Anchovies. Ellie's still not with them.

Neither is the Blond Caveman.

A slither of unease works its way down my spine. Not because I'm worried Ellie still has feelings for him, but because I don't trust him.

Especially when Mrs. Dixon's face lights up at the sight of the Ryders. "Michelle! Christopher! How lovely to see you both again."

She leans in for cheek kisses with Mrs. Ryder and to embrace Mr. Ryder.

Behind her back, Monica rolls her eyes so hard her tongue sticks out, and I realize maybe I'm not so bad.

All I want is a little love and acceptance.

These people, though—they're in it for the social status.

"How *is* the environmental business?" Mr. Dixon asks, engaged for the first time all week.

Mr. Ryder shakes his hand. "Good, good."

"You know our bank will be *more* than happy to help you out anytime you want to get out of that old neighborhood you're still living in. Upstanding family like yours should be in a house fitting your station."

Jason sighs.

Even Sloane seems surprised.

"We could never leave our home, but thank you," Mrs. Ryder informs them. She easily executes a side-step to hug Monica. "You look beautiful, sweetie. We're so happy for you two."

"I'm so glad you came," she replies.

When Mrs. Ryder turns to Monica's mom, I lean closer to the bride. "Where's Ellie?"

She points to a bench at the edge of the park, then frowns. "I think we pushed her too hard this week. She's limping. I told her to stay there, but—"

"Is she okay?" I ask at the same time Mr. Ryder asks, "But where is she *now*?"

"Miss Ellie kissed my daddy," Tucker announces.

Festival-goers keep passing by, a band of pirates leaps out into the middle of the street for an impromptu swordfight, and complete silence descends inside our group while the Ryders turn to look at me.

It's not that I didn't know this was coming.

Ever since the moment Ellie informed me that I owed her for ruining her wedding date, I've known I'd have to face her parents.

Her brother.

Our friends.

Explain it to Tucker.

"Oh, Wyatt!" Suddenly, Mrs. Ryder is squeezing me tight. "Oh, this is wonderful."

Mr. Ryder's grinning at me, and I've never felt so loved while hating myself quite so much at the same time, because soon enough we'll have to stage a break-up, and I don't know the next time I'll be able to look any of them in the eye.

"We should go find her," I say gruffly.

"Absolutely," Mr. Ryder agrees. He pulls his phone out and dials, and we all listen while the ringing rolls to voicemail.

Ellie's safe here. She can take care of herself, and the locals know her well enough that if she gets into trouble, or gets hurt, they'll be right at her side. She probably had to find a bathroom.

Or she went for banana pudding.

But the Blond Caveman is missing too.

I scan the square with its upturned dirt and more festival-goers digging for gold, the benches around it, up and down the sidewalk, but I don't spot her.

"Tucker, you want to hang with me?" Monica asks him, like she knows I'm about to head off to find her.

"Is that your real hair?" Tucker asks.

She nods and squats in her huge colonial princess dress, tilting her ringlets at him. "It sure is. Want to touch it?"

I don't want to leave him here. I have no idea what the Ryders will think of me when this week's over, and so I'm clinging to the one thing I know I'll still have.

But he drops my hand to inspect Monica's hair, and somebody needs to find Ellie.

Mr. Ryder inclines his head back toward the Crusty Nut. I nod and take off into the dug-up square and toward the bench Ellie was last seen sitting on.

I've barely passed the back edge of the building to my left when I hear voices.

Familiar voices.

"Why are you doing this to me?" the Blond Caveman demands.

"It's not *about* you, Patrick. This week is about Jason. And Monica."

"I meant shoving that asshole in my face."

There's a beat of silence before Ellie asks, "What are you talking about?"

"You, all over that jerkoff friend of your brother's."

I turn the corner and spot them. He's blocking her against a dumpster, and I'm about to say something when Ellie speaks.

"Your insecurities and delusions are not my problem. You don't get an opinion here. Now *move*."

"You're not listening to me—"

"And I don't have to. *We're done*. We've been done. Your opinion has no bearing on my life. Shut up and *let me go*."

"I'd do what she's asking," I interrupt. "She has a mean right hook."

I don't add *so do I*, because I don't actually make a habit of punching people, so all I have are gut instincts and the over-whelming desire to protect and defend what's mine.

And by *mine*, I mean my *family*.

And no, I don't want to talk about the way my heart is pounding or my muscles tensing to leap, because I will move fucking heaven and earth and travel to the depths of hell to make sure Ellie's safe—physically, mentally, emotionally, spiritually, all of it.

Safe. Sound. In one piece.

Fuck.

Fuck.

I'm in love with Ellie Ryder.

The Blond Caveman has four inches on me, but I will flatten him if I have to. And based on the curled-lip scowl under his powdered wig and the way he's flexing his arms under his vintage navy uniform, he's thinking he'd be happy to take me out too.

His lips part. "Shut your—"

"Your parents are here," I tell Ellie.

She smiles, and *fuck*, she's pretty.

It's not the colonial dress or the funny wig with long black curls either. It's the way she doesn't hold back on letting the smile spread cheek-to-cheek. The warmth in her eyes. The stubborn set of her shoulders.

Pretty?

No.

She's fucking *everything*. The whole package.

"They must be disappointed," the Blond Caveman sneers.

"That I'm happier without you? Not really." She leans toward me, and I wrap an arm around her shoulders while she slips away from him. Her pulse is fluttering fast in her neck, and I want to lay him out just on principle.

And then I want to carry her to the nearest dark corner and inspect every inch of her to make sure she's okay.

And then I want to kiss her. *Fuck*, I want to kiss her.

"Let's go," she says to me.

"Your girlfriend know what you're doing?" I ask the Blond Caveman while I twist so I'm between him and Ellie.

"She knows I defend helpless women, and she thinks it's hot."

Ellie chokes on air. I'm suddenly unable to stop a snicker.

"What the *fuck* are you laughing at?" he snarls.

"We better go quick," I mutter to Ellie. "You okay?"

She leans on me while we hasten back into view of the street, and it's going to hurt like hell when I can't touch her anymore.

"I was such an idiot," she sighs.

She's limping more than usual. Not good.

"How heavy is your wig?" I ask her. "Is that what I smell?"

"You're probably smelling your own armpits," she says, but she looks up at me and smiles with none of the old *you irritate the shit out of me* that's always been there.

No, this is *I love flirting with you.*

It's fucked-up flirting, but that's what it is, isn't it?

Flirting.

That's what it's always been.

We were just too stubborn to see it.

Or to admit it.

And no small part of me wishes we could go back to that.

Because leaving Ellie Ryder?

This is going to suck.

TWENTY-TWO

Ellie

BY THE TIME we're doing our last-minute hair and makeup fixes in a small tent just down the hill from the gazebo at the far end of Blackbeard Avenue where Monica and Jason will take their vows, I can't decide whose mother is happier—Monica's, or mine.

Definitely *not* Mrs. Dixon. She's getting an artsy-fartsy daughter-in-law from her black sheep son while her favorite son's girlfriend has been giving him the cold shoulder all afternoon.

But mine?

She's in utter heaven over me and Wyatt dating.

Next week just might kill her.

This isn't good.

"Jeez, Mom, maybe you should've adopted Wyatt and kicked me and Beck to the curb," I tell her while she fusses over my short curls. Any minute now, Pop's going to call us up for the wedding.

She swats my arm. "You hush. You know I love all my children equally. Wyatt just needed me more than you, Beck, and the rest of the boys and girls."

I'd be offended, but we were raised by a village. I was just as likely to get grounded by Mrs. Rivers as I was by my own mom. "He's lucky he had you," I tell her, and crap.

Now she's crying, and it's going to make me cry too, but not out of happiness and joy.

No, my tears will be all guilt.

And possibly grief, because Wyatt isn't an asshole, and he isn't a thorn in my side, and I don't know what to call him, but the *fake* part of *fake boyfriend* feels more wrong than the *boyfriend* part.

Which is impossible, because we really would die, and Tucker deserves to grow up with a good father.

"Stop, stop," Monica says, bustling over to hug her. She's changed from her colonial gown to a pirate wedding gown, an eclectic mix of formal and buccaneer, with pirate boots under her lacy hoop skirt and a leather corset embroidered with skulls and crossbones for her bodice. She has a bandana over her ringlets and giant hoop earrings dangle to her shoulders. "No crying until you hear the vows. They're beautiful. Ellie, how's your leg? Do you want me to send one of the Rock boys for a chair?"

"I'm *fine*," I tell her.

Okay, maybe I'm not *quite* as fine as that, but I can make it through the wedding before I need to lay myself up for a week to recover.

Alone.

Probably here in Shipwreck, because even without a dishwasher, Beck's house is still super comfortable, and it has internet, and I can borrow the laptop Mom brought to telework for a week.

The house will be weirdly empty, but it'll be nice to be alone again.

All alone.

With no one to talk to.

No one to poke. No one to share banana pudding with.

No little voices shrieking with laughter over bubbles or drawings of pirates or parrots, or asking to share a donut.

No one to kiss and cause the house to collapse around us with.

Dammit, I can't stop this weepy-eyed stuff.

"Monica, honey, it's time," her mom whispers.

Monica squeals, and her eyes go shiny too. "Oh my god, I'm marrying Jason," she whispers.

I squeeze her in a hug. "I'm so happy for you."

"Go on, go walk the plank—I mean, walk the aisle so I can get hitched."

My mom scurries to join Dad, Wyatt, and Tucker in a row of seats near the gazebo. The list of invited guests is small—a few friends and coworkers from Copper Valley, and a few aunts, uncles, and cousins on both sides—but the people of Shipwreck have turned out in force to watch.

And participate, though most of the guests and tourists who are also gathered beyond the reserved seating don't know that yet.

Mr. Dixon escorts Mrs. Dixon down the plank—I mean, aisle. Then Grady Rock escorts Monica's mom. And then it's time for Patrick, fully costumed as a member of the English Royal Guard, to walk me down the aisle.

I tuck my hand into his elbow, but while his powdered wig amuses me, I keep as much distance as physically possible while smiling at Jason, who's standing with Pop on the gazebo steps.

"We don't have to be like this," Patrick mutters.

I keep smiling. "There's no *we*, and if you don't shut up, I'm telling your girlfriend *you* dumped *me*, since I know she thinks it was the other way around."

He blanches.

We reach the gazebo and I gladly drop his arm. Wyatt's scowling. My dad doesn't look very pleased either.

But then the pirate band—yes, the pirate band—strikes up "Here Comes the Bride," and everyone rises as Monica emerges from the tent.

"Oh, god, she's gorgeous," Jason says hoarsely.

He's utterly adorable in his first mate getup. *We all know who's going to captain the ship of our life*, he told Monica when they were discussing formal wedding wear. *I'm wearing the first mate outfit.*

Monica's mom is already crying. Mine's dabbing her eyes in the next row back.

I wonder what Wyatt's thinking about while he watches my best friend walk down the aisle.

His own wedding?

Or maybe Tripp's, which was utterly gorgeous and completely opposite of this small-town pirate affair, because when a former boy bander marries a Hollywood A-lister, you're damn right it's spectacular.

But he glances back at me, and I'm suddenly quite certain he's not thinking about weddings at all.

There's something raw and unguarded and beautiful in his gray eyes. Regret mixed with hope.

My belly dips to my toes, adding an extra shiver to my bones along the way.

I like Wyatt Morgan.

I like Wyatt Morgan.

He's loyal. He's protective. He's smart. He's brave.

He adores that perfect, sweet, happy little boy fidgeting next to him.

He's a survivor.

Wounded in his soul, but still *here*. A good friend to my brother. The son my mother would've added to her household in a heartbeat.

The man who pushed me to be better since he got his own footing in the neighborhood.

Jason kisses Monica's cheek as she joins him on the gazebo steps. "Now, now, save that for marriage, boy," Pop says, and everyone laughs.

I take her bouquet—a red rose, a black rose, and a purple rose, tied together with a Jolly Roger ribbon and stuck in a rum bottle—and step back to let the wedding begin.

I might get a little teary-eyed too. The way Jason's just watching Monica, like he's the luckiest first mate to ever board a ship, like the only thing he needs in his life is her... Just *swoon*.

Thank you for finding me my missing puzzle piece, Monica told me once not long after I introduced them. But these two, I'm certain, would've found each other one way or another.

They were meant to be.

Wyatt's watching me. I can feel his gaze.

And it's not annoying, or haughty, or critical.

It's *hot*.

And not just *he wants to see me naked* hot. But *he feels it too* hot.

Monica and Jason say their vows. Monica's mom cries. My mom cries. I cry.

Tucker cries, because, "Dad, I don't like it when people cry."

Everyone laughs, and I wish I could hug Tucker the way Wyatt is now, just scooping him up and patting his back. "It's happy tears," I hear him murmur.

"I don't like it when you cry either," Jason tells Monica.

She wipes her eyes as she laughs. "It's joy leaking out my soul."

Joy.

They have joy.

I've always had plans. Calendars. Deadlines. Tasks. Life events to check off.

Maybe what I really need is *joy*.

Laughing with someone when the dishwasher leaks. When he accidentally sits on a squirt bottle of French dressing. When we knock heads in the middle of an orgasm.

I glance at Wyatt again.

Joy.

Oh my god.

He's my joy.

My laughter.

My strength.

My challenge.

My motivation.

My rock.

My joy.

His eyes are misty too, but he doesn't look away.

I suddenly don't care if I can never get pregnant or give birth.

I don't care if I never have a big wedding.

I don't care if nothing on the outside looks perfect.

I just don't want Wyatt to leave tomorrow.

"The rings!" Pop calls.

My mom gasps. Tucker leaps to his feet and points past the

gazebo. Wyatt's eyes leave mine, and they go comically wide. He starts to his feet too.

My dad's jaw is flapping.

I turn to look, already smiling, because I know what's coming, except—

"*Goats?*"

Monica shoots me a look and laughs like I'm crazy, but then her eyes, too, go round as a ship's wheel.

Because there's an army of goats cresting the hill and charging the gazebo.

The wedding guests are laughing.

So are the tourists.

But the locals who are in on all the wedding plans?

They're not.

Grady looks at me and mouths, *Goats?*

I shrug, because I don't know where they came from.

"The rings!" Monica says to Pop, who's also staring in surprise at the herd.

"The rings," he agrees.

Only Jason seems amused.

Confused, but also amused.

Pretty sure real pirates could invade his home and he'd just stand there watching. Unless they tried to take Monica as part of their booty.

Then I think things would get ugly.

Patrick hands Pop the rings.

A goat barrels into the gazebo from behind, darts across, and head-butts Pop's knee.

"Oh, no, you didn't, you little sucker!" Grady yells. "*Charge!* That powder monkey's making away with our pirate captain!"

"Little fucker. Little fucker," Long Beak Silver improvises from atop the gazebo.

"Dad—" Tucker says.

"I know. Don't repeat it," Wyatt tells him.

"The pirates—" Tucker says, pointing.

Sit, I mouth.

He narrows his eyes at me while two dozen locals dressed

like pirates charge up the aisle and around the chairs toward the bride and groom, yelling and waving swords.

I grin back at him.

And then a goat rams my left leg, and I gasp and buckle.

"With this ring, I thee wed!" Monica yells.

"With this ring, I thee wed!" Jason yells back.

I know he's supposed to unsheathe his sword and battle the pirates, but stars are dancing in my vision as a goat jumps on my knee and tries to lick my ears.

"I now pronounce you pirate and wife!" Pop yells.

"Back, you little fucker." Wyatt sweeps the goat back, and then I'm up in his arms. My dad's right behind us.

"Ellie. Hospital. Now," my dad orders.

"It's *fine*," I say.

I want to watch the show.

And grip Wyatt a little tighter.

And, yes, probably pop a painkiller—the over-the-counter kind, because I'm sure the pain will recede soon—or maybe two.

"Dad, the goat's licking me and the pirates are fighting," Tucker laughs.

"The swords!" I gasp. "Wyatt, the guests need their swords!"

"I got 'em, Ellie," Sloane calls.

And she does.

She's handing out foam swords to all of Jason and Monica's friends, who are leaping into the fray and battling the pirates who are trying to weave around the herd of goats to get to Monica.

"Back, you scurvy dogs!" Jason yells. "You'll never take my bride! Piracy can't stop true love! Only *death* can do that!"

"My hero," Monica cries happily.

He scoops her over his shoulder as Sloane throws me a sword. "Behind you!"

She hasn't given one to Patrick.

And he has four locals surrounding him.

"Babe, some help?" he says.

"Eat shit and die, you cheating asshole," she replies.

Mr. and Mrs. Dixon gasp in horror.

And that's before Grady's younger cousins attack them with foam swords. "Plunder the booty!" one of them yells.

I bash foam swords with Tillie Jean, defending Wyatt while he tries to get us out of the mess of goats and pirates.

"Tucker! Careful!"

"I've got him, Wyatt," Mom calls. "He's a good pirate fighter. You get Ellie to safety!"

She bops Grady on the head with the butt of her foam sword, and he staggers dramatically, trips over a wooden folding chair, and faceplants in the ground.

"Oh my god!" I gasp.

"He'll be fine," Tillie Jean says while I continue to fight her behind Wyatt's back. "The only person I know with a thicker skull than Grady is Cooper."

My dad stabs Tillie Jean in the back with his foam sword, and she makes a dramatic pirate death too, yelling, "My brothers in pirate arms are coming for you, Captain Monica!" as she croaks out her fake last breaths.

"Good one, Dad!" I call.

"*Safety*," he replies pointedly as he turns to help Mom defend Tucker against two more local pirates and the random goats.

Everyone's laughing.

Wyatt's dodging goats and tourists, not breaking a sweat, not even breathing hard as he carries me down behind Jason, who's running with Monica tossed over his shoulder. They're both laughing in glee, and I wonder if they'll still go straight to The Grog for the reception, or if they'll be fashionably late to their own party.

Probably late.

I take advantage of the fact that Wyatt's supposed to be my boyfriend to bury my face in his neck.

It's pretend, universe. Don't strike us with lightning, I plead.

Fuck, he smells good.

"Thank you for being my hero," I whisper against his hot skin.

"Thank you for letting me." His voice is thick, and he knows.

He feels it too.

The inevitable.

Destiny.

The reason he moved in on our street when we were little.

The reason we've always irritated each other.

The reason he was just out of reach when I finally noticed him.

Because it's been building up to this moment.

This exact moment here.

When he can be my hero.

And I can finally let him.

"Ellie?" he says thickly.

"Mm?"

"I don't want to let you go."

My heart swells three sizes and glows, radiating every ounce of affection I've ever denied having for this stubborn, strong, dependable man. "Your arms will eventually fall off," I whisper. "But you'll still be my hero even if they do."

"I'm going to miss you."

While Jason hustles Monica toward the Shipwreck Inn, Wyatt turns us down a side street and into a small public garden. He yanks on the wrought iron gate, and it shuts us inside with a *clink.*

"Are you kidnapping me?" I ask breathlessly.

"I'm seizing the moment."

The Shipwreck Gardens are small—it's more like *garden,* singular, surrounded with an ivy-covered wall, a fountain featuring a statue of Thorny Rock and his pirate treasure chest standing proudly in the center.

Wyatt sets me gently on a bench with my back to the shops on Blackbeard Avenue, so I can see the roofs of the town's cozy houses beyond, and the gently sloped, blue haze-covered mountain peaks around us, and he squats on one knee in front of me.

My eyes bulge.

At least, until he ducks his head and laughs. "God, Ellie, it's so easy."

"You—you—" I sputter, but then I'm laughing with him.

Laughing and cradling his head as he laughs right there in my lap, over the crazy colonist dress I wore for Monica because I would've gone to her wedding dressed as a half-naked mermaid if she'd asked me to.

"How's your leg?" Wyatt asks as we both regain control.

"Oh, it aches like a mother," I reply cheerfully.

"Overdid it?"

"Times ten."

He rubs his hand softly over my thigh through the fabric. "What do you need?"

"Warm bath, Motrin, and rum." My fingers rest on his shoulders, just enough contact to make me feel grounded. "And maybe more of that."

"This?" He tests the pressure on my muscle, and I sigh and nod.

"Is it supposed to still ache?"

"Muscle and nerve damage on top of newly healed bone. Eventually it'll probably only be bad with weather changes, but apparently broken hips and femurs like to take their sweet time to heal."

"No crutches?"

"I graduated crutches early, thank you."

His lips twitch while he watches me with those intense gray eyes. "You're a fighter."

"I'm tired of fighting," I whisper.

His gaze searches mine like he's asking if I'm tired of fighting the pain, or tired of fighting him. "That's just because you know you'll never have a cooler wedding," he whispers back.

My jaw drops a split second before the laughter overtakes me. "You are such a—such a—" I gasp out, searching for the right name to call him.

"Stud," he supplies with an eyebrow wiggle, and it's so *un*-Wyatt-like that I double over in laughter.

Except doubling over puts my face right next to his, and he's smiling, his eyes alive and happy and twinkling with utter mischief, and *this* is everything.

He's everything.

Everything I never knew I wanted, wrapped up in one Wyatt-shaped package.

I don't know who starts the kiss, but once his lips are on

mine, I know I won't be the one to break it. He's still massaging my leg while he loops his free hand behind my neck. I cling to his polo shirt, and almost laugh into the kiss thinking how crazy the two of us must look.

Him dressed like he's a tourist from this century, me decked out like some kind of island colonist from the 1700s, a baby goat bleating beside us...

It's the goat that breaks us apart.

Mostly because I can't laugh and kiss him at the same time.

I need more practice.

More time.

"Ellie?" he says softly through a chuckle.

"Hmm?"

"I'm going to make love to you, and the world's not going to end."

"That's a terrible idea," I choke out.

"Challenge accepted."

TWENTY-THREE

Wyatt

THE LIST of reasons I shouldn't be playing with the hem of Ellie's skirt is longer than my arm. Tucker could catch us here. Ellie's parents. The baby goat that got through the gate could try to help. Someone else could walk into the gardens.

I could get in serious trouble and lose my job for indecent exposure.

But when Ellie's only objection to me snaking my hands up under her skirt is that *we're tempting fate,* I run my hands over her knees and up her thighs.

She shudders and widens her legs as her lids get heavy. "We're not supposed to do this," she whispers.

"I like you," I whisper back, "and I want to make you feel good."

"I take no responsibility for your son becoming an orphan," she informs me.

I have zero fear that her belief that we're physically dangerous is accurate. It's superstitious nonsense, and it's not like Ellie to believe in it. "What are you really afraid of?"

I don't expect her to answer me, so I dip my thumbs low on her inner thighs. She's not flinching away from letting me touch her scars, and I wish I could kiss her where she hurts and make it go away.

Her eyes squeeze closed as her legs fall open wider. "I'm afraid I'm not lovable."

My heart cracks in two.

I didn't know I had it in me for my heart to crack for another person, but it did. Split. Right in half like someone attacked it with a rusty butter knife.

"Why?"

"I'm stubborn."

"Determined," I correct.

"Annoying."

"Says who?"

"*You.*"

"Only to get your goat."

The baby goat bleats again, and her lips wobble upward. But her eyes—*Christ.*

Her eyes are breaking my heart. "I'm too career-minded."

"You have a calling."

"I didn't pick it."

"Didn't have to."

Her skin is so soft, and I can smell her arousal through the layers of her dress.

"I don't know what's important," she insists. "I can't prioritize people over *things.* I don't know how to let go and trust someone else. I can't—"

"You're Ellie Fucking Ryder. Yes, you can."

"Why do you believe in me?"

"Mostly to piss you off." I wink at her and stroke the edge of her panties, and she huffs out a smile and a groan.

"*Wyatt.*"

"Come see me in Georgia."

"What?"

"Come see me. Me and Tucker. Spend the weekend with us. In two weeks. Three weeks. Whenever you have a free weekend. Come see us."

She blinks quickly, but not fast enough to erase the sheen in her eyes. "Why?"

"Because I'm going to fucking miss you." Honesty makes my voice raw. I never thought I'd get married. Never trusted that I could fall in love and know how to do it right.

But Ellie?

She won't let me do it wrong.

Because she's Ellie. She'll push me. She'll teach me. And if she'll love me, she'll *love* me.

"Wyatt," she whispers, and then her hands clasp around my ears and she's kissing me.

Softly.

So softly.

Like she's learning me. Memorizing me.

Savoring me.

I stroke the center of her panties, and her groan vibrates against my lips. I stroke her again, and she arches into my touch while she nips my lower lip. "More," she says into our kiss.

So I give her more, stroking and teasing and touching her while we kiss, slow and easy, then slow and deep, then hard and desperate while she jerks against my fingers. I slip two under her panties, find her entrance, and thrust into her slick heat.

But it's not enough.

I don't want to just feel her.

I want to taste her.

"Wyatt," she gasps when I duck under her skirts. "We're— someone could—*ohmygod do it again*."

I push her panties aside, put my mouth to her pussy, and I devour her sweet center. Her hips buck into my mouth, and *fuck*, I could stay here all day.

I don't care that I can't see a fucking thing. I don't care that it's hot as hell.

I don't even care that we could get caught at any minute.

I just know I'm finally right where I'm supposed to be.

Loving Ellie.

Pleasuring her.

Her gasps are muffled, but she's holding my head steady through her skirt, urging me higher, left, *right there oh my god more right there suck me harder Wyatt yes harder YES*.

I slide two fingers deep inside her hot, wet channel, and when my lips find her sweet little nub, I nip gently, then suck it, and she's suddenly clamping around my fingers, her thighs squeezing my head while she comes for me.

"*Yes,*" she gasps. "Wy-aa-aah-"

I tense, and sure enough—

"*Ah-choo!*"

Her walls clench tight around my fingers again, spasming harder and coating me, and fuck if her coming doesn't make me about to blow my own load in my pants.

"Fuck," she mutters, but it comes out on a half-groan while her pussy's still coming for me.

She sneezes once more, and I pull my fingers out, gently replace her panties, and peek out from under her dress.

"*Baaah!*' the baby goat bleats.

Ellie's wiping her nose with her arm. Her cheeks are rosy, her body slumping on the bench.

"It was messy," she grumbles, pointing to her nose. "And we're probably going to get eaten by baby goats in our sleep. But thank you. That was the best orgasm I've had in years."

I frown. "So I have work to do to be the best ever."

She sniffles. "You really want to do this again?" she asks, gesturing to her snotty face with the healing black eye.

God, she's gorgeous. And so very *Ellie.*

"Yes," I tell her. "Preferably soon. And often."

The hesitation in her bright blue eyes wavers, and then she's laughing again, leaning in to kiss me. "You know something worse than goats will happen now, right?"

I grip her chin. "Nothing. Bad. Is. Going. To. Happen."

One eye wrinkles.

"I like you, Ellie Ryder." *I love you, but I don't want to scare you.*

"I like you too, Wyatt Morgan."

"Then don't be afraid." I lean in to kiss her again when we hear the gate rattle.

She jerks back, and I straighten too when I recognize that voice.

"But I want to show you the fountain!" Tucker says.

"Leg better?" I ask her.

She smiles softly. "Nature's miracle cure worked."

"See? That's not bad."

"Hmm."

I can still taste her on my lips, and I'm more than a little sore and eager in other parts of my very unsatisfied anatomy, but I take a seat next to her, cross my ankle over my knee, and fling an arm around her shoulder while the gate creaks open.

She glances at my crotch, then back up to my face. "Not going to complain?"

"About getting to eat you? No. Are you going to complain about it?"

"No," she replies with a smile.

"Good. But I'm sneaking into your bed tonight after your parents are asleep."

"Are you?" she murmurs as Tucker races into the garden and spots us.

"Yep. And I can't wait."

She lays her head on my shoulder as her parents follow Tucker, who's talking a mile a minute about the goats and the pirates and the wedding and acting out a sword fight.

"This isn't fake anymore, is it?" she whispers.

"No, ma'am," I whisper back into her wig.

And I'm not sure it ever was.

TWENTY-FOUR

Ellie

MONICA AND JASON'S party at The Grog is more fun than I've had in months. Possibly years. There are pirate jokes and impromptu sword fights and a limerick contest with a bunch of implied words to protect the innocent ears in the room. Tucker makes friends with Monica's cousin's daughter, who's a year younger than he is, and the two of them spend the evening playing pirate and talking about Pokémon cards and video games.

Nobody talks about work or where we'll be next week, except Monica and Jason, who will be on a cruise in the Bahamas.

My parents want to know about when Wyatt and I hooked up though.

"A psychic set us up," he says, which makes my mom spit her ale.

"I watched him lift a burning car off a baby and decided he was okay," I say, which is lame after his answer, but Mom stops the third degree, and I find I can breathe again.

I don't mean to rub my leg, but it's aching after coming down off my post-orgasm high, and suddenly Monica's next to us. "If you don't take her home and get her a hot bubble bath and a glass of wine *right now*, I'm going to ask the Rocks to blacklist you from Crow's Nest *and* Anchovies," she informs Wyatt.

"It's your wed—" I start, but she clamps her arm around my head and her hand across my mouth and gives Wyatt the *I'm watching you* hand gesture, then points to the door.

"We both have cars here," I say, but it comes out as "ee owe aah rrr rr" with Monica's hand still over my mouth.

If it weren't her wedding day, I'd lick her hand, but honestly, I don't know where it's been, and I like Jason, but I don't want to accidentally lick his penis sweat.

"We'll drive your car back, sweetie," Mom says.

"It's like she doesn't know you at all," Wyatt whispers. "Sweetie?"

Monica snorts with laughter.

So does my father.

"I'll go get Tucker," Wyatt says to Monica.

"Oh, we'll bring him home," my mom says quickly. "He's having so much fun."

He's drinking root beer and completely missing all of his dart throws, which is about the cutest thing I've seen all day.

"Out! *Out!*" somebody suddenly crows. One of the wandering goats has wandered into the bar.

"Goats a normal part of the festival?" Wyatt asks.

Grady Rock pauses on his way to the animal and shakes his head. "Never. Don't know where the damn—darn things came from."

"They're homeless goats?" Dad asks.

Grady leans down and gets it by its horns. "Or somebody over in Sarcasm sent them," he mutters.

"Wouldn't they have unicorn horns if Sarcasm sent them?" I ask.

He glares at me. "You're lucky you're cute, or you'd be really annoying."

"They could be wild goats," Wyatt points out. "Nomadic mountain goats. Psychic nomadic mountain goats come down to make sure you don't call very nice women *annoying*."

Mom coughs to cover a laugh when Grady pins him with a

look. "So let's move the goats to your bedroom and see how you feel."

"Aren't they the cutest, Chris? We should take one home," Mom says to Dad.

"Nomadic mountain goats wouldn't take well to domestication," he replies.

"Dad! Dad! Can we keep a goat?" Tucker barrels over, wedding cake frosting on his cheek. I wipe it off while Wyatt shakes his head.

"Your mother would kill me. You ready to go, or do you want to stay a while? I have to take Miss Ellie home."

Tucker frowns at me. "Does your leg hurt, Miss Captain Ellie?"

"Just a little," I tell him.

"I got a cut on my finger." He shoves the digit an inch from my nose, and I draw back to peer at the pinprick-size dot of red on his middle finger.

"Did you get in a sword fight with toothpicks?" I ask.

His eyes go wide. "How did you know?"

"That's how I get all my best cuts."

"Tucker?" Wyatt asks.

"I wanna stay. Me and Sophia's gonna play darts some more and pet the goats."

Grady groans as he wrestles one goat out, but two more come in.

"You be good for Mr. and Mrs. Ryder, understand?"

"Yeah, Dad!"

He catches the little boy by the hips before he can dart away. "And when they say it's time to go, it's time to go. Yes, sir?"

"Yes, sir. Can I go play darts now?"

"Hug first."

Tucker launches himself at Wyatt and squeezes. "Love you, Dad."

"Love you too, bud."

He scampers off, and Wyatt shoots a look at my parents. "He's a little sugared up."

"Psh. I raised Beck. I can handle Tucker on a little sugar." She and Wyatt trade keys so we don't have to swap Tucker's booster seat.

"I'm becoming displeased," Monica says.

"Want me to toss them, babe?" Jason asks.

"Yes."

"We're going," Wyatt tells them, pulling me to my feet. He frowns, and shakes his head as he looks at me. "Nope. Not that way."

"What—" I start, but before I can finish, he's hefted me over his shoulder again like a sack of potatoes.

"Leg okay?" he asks.

"This is really annoying."

"I'm so tempted to slap your ass, but that would be a bad example for my kid."

"And my parents are watching."

"I know. Your dad's glaring at me."

I manage to shuffle around until I can see my dad's upside-down face.

And Dad's not glaring.

Nope.

If anything, he's watching me like he's realized his baby girl is all grown up. "Drive careful," he says gruffly to Wyatt.

"Always," Wyatt replies.

And despite that lingering fear that something terrible is waiting around the corner, because *holy hell*, that was quite the orgasm Wyatt gave me before the reception, I'm not the least bit concerned about making it back up to the house safe and sound.

It's Wyatt.

Dependable, reliable, smokin' hot, *likes me* Wyatt.

"I'm sorry I didn't call you back," I tell him as we leave The Grog.

He doesn't ask *when*.

Nope.

"You needed your energy to kick recovery's ass," he replies.

I could argue that I owed him an hour of my time. That it wasn't nice of me to let him worry. Or any other argument in the world.

Instead, I murmur, "Speaking of asses…." and take advantage

of being carried over his shoulder, which puts me in a great spot to not only ogle his, but also squeeze it.

His pace speeds up, and there I go again, laughing.

I haven't laughed this much in ages.

And all it took was learning not to hate Wyatt.

Who knew?

TWENTY-FIVE

Ellie

WE RIDE in companionable silence up to the house.

Holding hands.

While my heart pounds in my throat.

Everything's different, but it's also *right*.

Wyatt knows my cranky sides. My stubborn sides. My ugly sides. He knows what he's in for.

And he wants it anyway.

Despite who I am at my worst.

And he's not pretending to be anyone he's not either. I know *this* side of Wyatt. I've seen him with my brother. With the other guys we grew up with. With their sisters.

With Tucker.

Even with Lydia.

The difference is, he doesn't hold back with me.

He lets me see his ugly sides too.

He's barely turned the car off in the garage before I lean across and grab him by the shirt and pull him in for a kiss.

I've always hated that Wyatt always seems to know exactly how to do everything.

That hatred does *not* extend to how well he kisses.

No, I'm seriously enjoying that right now. From my roots to my toes. Every bit of me is lit up, turned on, and ready.

"Ellie," he gasps, pulling back. "Inside."

"Race you."

"Okay, gimpy."

"Oooh, you—"

I cut myself off, because he's flinging open the car door, and there is no way I'm not even putting up a fight.

Or maybe I'll fight dirty.

"Wyatt? I don't think I can walk by myself."

I bat my eyelashes.

He snorts with laughter.

I grin.

And he circles the car to pull me out. We stand toe-to-toe, belly-to—huh.

"That's not your belly," I whisper.

He looks down between us. "No, it's not."

"So it's not some kind of intestinal protrusion either?"

"You are a pain in the ass," he says with a laugh, and then I'm up in his arms—*not* over his shoulder, but cradled close to his chest while I loop my fingers together behind his neck.

I press a kiss to the pulsing vein under his rugged jawline.

"You don't suck at that," he says huskily, so I kiss him again. Except this time I graze my teeth over the throbbing vein and follow it with a quick swipe of my tongue.

He stumbles through the door and puts me on the ground. "Do you know what I need?" he growls.

I arch my belly into his hard length. "I have an idea."

He nods. "That's right. Strip darts."

My eyes jerk wide, and he grins. "C'mon, Ellie. You've gotta *earn* this body."

"Oh, those are fighting words," I say, my own smile growing in direct proportion to the arousal pinging through my veins.

Strip darts.

This is going to be fun.

I take the lead, ignoring the twinge and fatigue in my leg to pull him down the hall and around the corner into the game room. I hit the lights, and he instantly turns the knob to dim them.

"Ah, a real challenge," I say softly, drawing my fingertips down the corded muscles on his forearms. "Throwing pointy objects in the dark."

"Guess you'll have to trust me not to miss."

I let him grab the darts out of the board while I lean against the pool table, and when he returns, he hands me the set. "Ladies first."

"Oh, no, I'm much more motivated at seeing what I'm working toward. Gentlemen first."

The challenge in his smile is pure Wyatt, but it's also…*more*.

"Rules?" I ask.

"One of us gets a bullseye, the other takes something off."

"And one of us misses, we take something off."

"In a hurry?"

"With the way you play darts, I'd never get my shoes off if I had to wait for you to hit a bullseye."

"Prepare to lose your socks, Ellie Ryder."

He throws his first dart, and it impales the wall six inches to the left of the board. "Bullseye," he declares.

I shriek with surprised laughter. He grins, and pulls off one shoe. "So close," he declares, and now I'm almost bent double.

His second dart gets closer to the board. "You're gonna be handing me those pantaloons next," he says while he kicks off his second shoe.

"*Pantaloons?*"

He gasps a mock gasp. "You're not wearing pantaloons? Ellie, did you go to your friend's wedding *commando*?"

"You know I didn't." But the idea of being commando, of being able to push him to the ground, straddle him, and take him inside me in an instant, is doing exactly what he wants it to do, and my panties are getting soaked again.

He grins like he knows it, and takes aim again.

This time, his dart doesn't even stick. It bounces off the Dogs Playing Poker poster two feet to the left of the board.

"Damn," he says, but he doesn't sound the least bit unhappy.

Nor does he look the least bit unhappy when he shucks his khaki shorts and stands there tenting his St. Patrick's Day boxers.

I'd laugh at the boxers, but there's nothing funny about how hard he is.

No, that's just plain intriguing. And arousing.

"You're up," he tells me, handing me my three darts.

"I'd say *you're* up."

"Recurring problem around you."

"My nipples are commiserating."

His eyes go dark. I turn to take my first throw, and he brushes my hair off my neck and presses a kiss to my nape.

Oversensitive aftershocks from his touch ripple across my skin. The dart doesn't even reach the wall.

"Do that again," I whisper.

"Ah-ah. You need to take something off first." His breath is hot on my ear, and he follows the chastising with a nip to my earlobe that has me whimpering in pleasure.

"Shoe," I say, holding out my foot for him.

He bends and obliges, pulling off my boot. "Cheater," I whisper when my sock comes off too.

"Just saving us some time when you miss again."

I line up for my shot, and he lines his erection up with the top of my ass, then dips his head to nibble at the crook of my neck while I fire the dart.

"Bullseye," I gasp.

"Bull*shit*," he says with a chuckle.

"But I hit the board."

"Barely. Gotta lose something, Ellie. It's the rules."

"Fine. You may remove my other shoe."

God, this is fun.

He obliges again, and this time, he doesn't let my foot go until he's kissed a path from my ankle bone to my knee.

"Cheating," I gasp.

"Well, yeah," he replies with another smokin' hot grin.

This is the side of Wyatt I've overlooked for years. The fun, playful side. He's always been obnoxious and buttoned up and stiff, *perfect* for a military career, but that's not all there is to him.

I could throw my last dart before he tries to distract me, but what's the fun in that?

And sure enough, as soon as he's straightened and behind me, his hands are on me again, this time high on my waist. "Need pointers?" he asks.

"I think you're already giving me pointers." I arch into the bulge against my lower back, and his breath hitches.

"I've been giving you pointers all day, but you haven't noticed."

"I've noticed."

"You gonna throw that last dart?"

"Debating if I want to hit a bullseye and make you lose the shirt." It's *so* freaking *right* here in his arms.

"Not the boxers?"

"I'm a big fan of anticipation."

"You're a big fan of torture."

"That too."

He nuzzles my neck again. I toss my last dart, and I don't even care where it landed, because now I can turn in Wyatt's arms and kiss him.

I know this might be a mistake, but if I don't have Wyatt, I'm going to die.

So I'll either die because the universe is a dick and doesn't like us together, or I'll die because I can't have him.

I'd rather go out happy, thank you very much.

"Want—you," I whimper into Wyatt's kiss.

"Never knew—needed you—so bad," he gasps between kisses as he tugs at the zipper on the back of my dress.

And I get a sudden chill, because this is where it started.

In a basement.

Without thought.

"Ellie?" Wyatt murmurs, his hand stilling.

"Can we really do this?"

"Yes."

"But *should* we?"

He threads his fingers through my hair and presses that thick bulge into my belly. "What are you afraid of?"

He asks it like whatever it is, he's going to leap onto his

magical unicorn and ride it into battle and slay my fears. "That we'll break," I whisper.

"Or maybe we'll finally get it right."

"What if the house burns down?"

I feel his smile against my lips. "The house is *not* going to burn down."

"How can you be sure?"

"Neither one of us were in the right headspace for this six months ago. But now? Today? You didn't look at your ex *once* during the reception. I wasn't there for *him*. I was there for *you*. Deny it."

I open my lips to do just that, but I realize he's right.

I forgot Patrick was even there.

"I just didn't want you to feel self-conscious."

He chuckle-snorts, and I giggle, because we both know I wouldn't stroke his ego.

However, my fingers are trailing down his pecs and abs looking for something else to stroke.

"Do I need to get a bullseye to get this dress off you?" he asks.

"No, you need to pull the fucking zipper down."

"Now?"

"Yes, please."

"Look at you, using your manners and everything." He tugs on the zipper once again, and cool air hits my back.

I push his shirt up, revealing that chest that I could spend days exploring, and my nipples pull so tight I feel it in my clit when he reaches behind himself with one hand to pull the shirt over his head and the rest of the way off.

He brushes my dress off my shoulders, and then I'm standing there, in just my panties, while he whispers my name in sheer reverence.

I step out of the puddle of fabric, and he snags it, tosses it on the pool table, then scoops me into his arms and lays me on it.

I tip my head back and laugh, because my brother would kill me if he knew what we were doing.

Wyatt hooks his thumbs in his boxers and pulls them off in one smooth motion, and all thoughts of anything except him flee my mind. He disappears, ducking beside the table, and I whimper.

"Condom," he says, returning to crawl onto the pool table with a foil packet in his hand.

"This thing won't break, will it? That would be awesome. Death by sex on a pool table."

"I got a private Bro Code show with this as their stage once," he replies. "It's solid."

"Ew. Maybe we should move to the foosball table. It's clean, right? Bumpy, but clean?"

"Have you met your brother? He licks his players for luck."

We both crack up.

But only until he dips his head to tease my nipple with his tongue.

Then nothing's funny.

But everything's perfect.

Right.

Glorious.

"My turn," I gasp when he pinches my other nipple. "Roll over."

"No."

"Wyatt—"

"I love that irritated note in your voice. It makes me so fucking hard."

I look down as he pushes up onto all fours, and *whoa*.

He's definitely hard.

"C'mon, Calamity Ellie. Tease me."

I push him onto his back and twist, and my stupid leg twinges. But before I can moan, Wyatt kisses me and gently caresses my leg and hip. "What's more comfortable for you? A bed?"

I shake my head, because dammit, I still want to be the kind of crazy that has sex on pool tables. And it's not the table. "I don't know. Just—I don't know how I bend best."

He grins like that's a challenge. "Then let's start with what we know works." He leans me back again and kisses me, and his long fingers trace a path over my hip to my panties.

I gasp as his knuckles graze the cotton over my clit.

"But you—haven't—not—"

"I have a few years of taunting you to make up for," he says as he moves to kiss a path down my jaw to that sweet, sensitive spot at the base of my throat.

"I was—you were—*oh, god, Wyatt.*"

"I'm going to take your panties off."

My *yes* comes out garbled as he peels the waistband down over my hips, taking special care around my scars, kissing my breasts, my belly, all the way down until he's nipping at my inner thigh.

My pussy's aching. "Touch me," I gasp, widening my right leg.

"Soon," he says, still pressing soft kisses on my sensitive skin. "*Now.*"

He kisses lower on my leg, heading for my knee. "If you're in that much of a hurry, maybe you should touch yourself."

He lifts hooded eyes to mine. *Touch yourself, Ellie. Turn me on by touching yourself.*

I hold his gaze while my fingers drift between my legs to stroke my slick folds. "Like this?" Oh, *god*, that feels good, but it's not enough.

"More," he rasps out.

I flick at my clit, and my legs open wider, because it's not enough. "I want *you*," I tell him.

"Say it again."

"I want you."

"Say my name."

"Wyatt, *I want you.*"

Finally, *finally*, he crawls back up my body until his sheathed length is pressing at my entrance. "Here?"

"*Yes.*"

"What about tomorrow?" he's teasing me, gliding his thick head along my seam. "Will you want me tomorrow?"

I grasp his cock and stroke him, and *oh*, so hard, like iron, and I can feel his pulse in the thick veins circling him. "Tomorrow— argue with you—at breakfast—over toast," I gasp. "Next week— fighting—who pays for dinner."

"And next month?" he asks, finally, *finally* inching inside me toward that needy emptiness that might be in my pussy or that might be in my soul, spreading me and teasing at how well he'll fill me when he gives me everything.

"Next month—surprise you—on a Tuesday—on my knees."

"Fuck, Ellie." He shoves deep inside me, and I cry out in relief at being connected to him. "I don't want to let you go."

"Then don't."

"You feel so fucking perfect."

He slowly pulls almost all the way out, then pushes back in again, hitting that *oh so perfect* sensitive spot deep inside me.

"Again," I gasp.

"Want you every day," he says as he thrusts into me again.

Every day. No one wants me every day. "You're craz—aa*aah*, oh god, Wyatt, *more*."

He thrusts again, not too gentle, not too hard, and the anticipation is building, the tension tightening, my pussy swelling and going hypersensitive with every stroke inside me.

"In my bed," he says.

"On the kitchen table."

"In the shower."

"In the backseat of your car."

"Under the stars."

"On top of the Eiffel Tower."

"In your parents' linen closet."

I laugh as he thrusts in again, and everything swirls out of focus while my climax hits hard. "*Ellie*," he cries, his dick pulsing inside me in time with my pussy squeezing and spasming around him.

"*Wyatt*," I gasp when he pumps once, twice more, pushing me higher and farther and deeper until— "Wy—ahh-*ahh*—"

He pushes up, his dick still straining deep inside me, and when I sneeze, he gasps. "Christ, Ellie, that feels amazing."

I'm still twitching and spasming around him, and here I am, laughing. "My *sneeze*?"

"Fuck, yeah." He drops his head into my shoulder, panting. "Was that it? I could take another sneeze. *Christ*."

I laugh, and another tingle of pleasure lights up my clit. "You're crazy."

"Crazy for you." He kisses my shoulder, my neck, up to my lips, where he lingers, lazily kissing me and letting me trace his jaw and stroke his short, soft hair. "I think I've wanted you my entire life. I was just too blind to realize it."

"Too scared," I whisper.

"That too."

"Are you still scared?"

He lifts his head, and serious Wyatt is back. "Depends. Were you serious about surprising me in Georgia with a blow job?"

I gape at him for half a second.

He cracks a grin.

"*You*—" I start, but he swallows my tirade with another kiss, and truly, kissing Wyatt is better than strawberry daiquiris on a beach.

I don't know what tomorrow will bring.

But I know one thing.

It will be the first day of the rest of my life with Wyatt.

TWENTY-SIX

Wyatt

ELLIE and I are fooling around in the master bathtub when the text comes in that the Ryders are on their way back with Tucker. She goes pink in the cheeks. "My parents know what we're doing," she whispers.

I kiss her forehead before I reach for a towel. "And they approve, because I'm awesome."

Her lips twitch. "Or maybe because they know I can keep you in line."

"Nah."

I'm smiling as I disentangle my legs from hers and climb out of the tub, and not just because her eyes go dark and smoky again as her gaze wanders down my dripping wet body.

No, it's because of the peace.

The utter contentment.

I never wanted to get married because I didn't think it was in my genes, in my bloodline, to be capable of being a good husband and father. Fate proved me wrong on fatherhood.

And this sensation that I've found a missing piece of myself, and that she's sitting right there in the bubble bath, turning down the music and tucking her hair behind her ear. "Did you grab my dress from downstairs?"

"It's on the bed."

"I didn't mean you had to. I could've gotten it. I just—"

I silence her with a kiss, which might be my new favorite hobby. Kissing Ellie Ryder.

Who knew?

"I left your shoes for you to get yourself," I tell her. "But I'll probably go get them anyway because you'll get mad and insist you're perfectly capable, and then we'll have some silly little fight that'll end with me needing to stroke your pussy, so—"

"Yep. Same old obnoxious Wyatt," she says with a grin.

"Same old stubborn Ellie."

She rests her hands on the edge of the tub and leans her chin on them, watching me dry off. "Provided we don't die, we're never going to be bored, are we?"

"I might be."

She gets me with a surprise slap to the ass, then shrieks as she slips under the water.

I give her to the count of one-half before I'm grabbing her arm and pulling her up.

"Okay?" I ask.

She blows and spits at the bubbles around her mouth. I grab my phone and angle it toward her like I'm going to snap a picture, and she rolls her eyes with a laugh. "Go ahead."

"Nah, I don't—"

"Oh, no. I want you to remember this for the rest of your life. Get in here. Selfie with me."

When I get down on my knee, she scoops bubbles onto my head and dribbles them on my nose.

And we're both smiling in the picture.

"Crazy woman." I wipe her face with the towel and set out another on the floor for her when she gets out. "You hungry?"

"You know what sounds good?"

"Banana pudding?"

"Tea. I have chamomile sometimes to help me fall asleep when I'm achy."

"With banana pudding?"

"We're out."

I put a hand to my heart and stagger. "You're right. We can't be together. We'll run out of banana pudding and die."

She throws the towel at me with a laugh. "Shush and go heat me some water, powder monkey."

"Yes, ma'am, Calamity Ellie."

While she takes her time getting out, I toss on sweatpants and a T-shirt, fill a tea kettle and turn on the burner, then head downstairs to get her shoes. Tucker's left his security blanket down here again, so I take it upstairs too, all the way to his bedroom, and pull out pajamas for him since he'll probably be dead on his feet at this hour.

Hope he had fun.

I'm on my way back downstairs when I smell it.

Smoke.

"Wyatt?" Ellie calls, and there's no mistaking the panic in her voice.

Nor the blare of the smoke alarms that suddenly explode in the house.

I tear down the stairs and land in a cloud of smoke just outside the kitchen. Ellie's in here, coughing, and flames are erupting from the stove. "The towel!" she shrieks, then coughs again.

Fuck.

I snag the flaming fabric and fling it in the sink, then turn the faucet on. "Get out," I tell her. The smoke's not too thick—I don't think anything else is burning—but the smoke alarms are still going off and the towel's still flaming in the sink.

I turned on the wrong fucking burner.

I turned on the wrong fucking burner.

And there was a fucking *towel* on it.

And I nearly burned Beck's house down.

After promising her *that would never happen.*

"Hi, yes, there's a fire," I hear her say. "It's at… Oh my god, I don't know the address. Beck's house. Beck–Beck—*what's my last name*? Yes! Beck Ryder's house. On the mount—*yes*!"

The alarms are screeching. She grabs my arm. "Wyatt. *Out*. Both of us. 9-1-1 says we have to get out. Now."

I spray the last of the embers and check the stove, which is off. "It's out, Ellie."

"*You are not going to die in a house fire on my watch, goddammit, get the fuck out!*" she shrieks.

She doubles over, coughing, then says, "Yes, we're still here," and that's when I hear it.

The high-pitched panic.

"Ellie—"

"*Out!*"

She's in a bathrobe, and she's limping hard. The haze isn't thick enough to mask it. "*Please* get out," she adds, and now there's a choked sob in her voice, and *fuck*.

I sweep her up and head for the door. "Okay. We're getting out. It's okay."

As soon as we're outside, she twists. "Let go."

Tears are streaming down her face.

"Ellie—"

"No. *No*. Don't. Back up." She retreats down the sidewalk to the driveway. The yard is too sloped for her to head there, and the limp is breaking me. "Yes, we're outside. We'll stay out."

She's crying.

Ellie's crying.

Ellie *never* cries. She tells those tears to back the fuck up and get out of her way.

But she's crying. On the phone with a 9-1-1 operator.

"It's my fault," she sobs. "I ignored the signs."

"Ellie. Stop."

Headlights flash up the driveway. The Ryders are back. They stop mid-way to the house, and Mrs. Ryder flies out of the passenger seat. "What happened? What's wrong?"

"We burned the house down," Ellie sobs, letting her mom gather her up while the alarm blares inside.

"We didn't—" I start, but my objection is cut off by the wail of a fire engine's siren in the distance.

"A fire?" Mr. Ryder asks.

"I set a towel on fire. It's out. It's fine. It was an accident."

"It's because we—we—"

"Ellie, it's not—"

Sometimes I wish my hair was long enough to pull it out, because that might help distract from the ice-cold fear settling into my chest.

Both the Ryders look at me, but Tucker leaps out of the car, fear written all over his little face, looking so fucking much like the kid I remember being at his age, and my throat closes up and my eyes sting and I grab him tight. "It's okay," I say as he starts to cry too.

"Miss Captain Ellie's crying," he sobs. "Is the house gonna burn down?"

"Hey, no, no, everything's fine." Everything's not fucking fine.

"Take me home," Ellie whimpers. "Mom? Take me home. I want to go home."

"Honey, it's late," Mr. Ryder says.

Headlights flash again, but instead of a firetruck, it's a fire engine red sports car.

Fucking *hell*.

"Ellie—" I start again while I hug my son and my best friend steps out of his car and the closest people I have left to parents gape at me in utter confusion.

"We *can't*, Wyatt," she says, her words muffled against her mom's shoulder but still clear as day to me. "We. Will. Die."

"We—"

"When's the last time you ever accidentally set a towel on fire? Never. *Ever.* Because it's you. *You don't make mistakes. We are not supposed to be together."*

"Ellie, sweetie, what's all this?" her mom says gently. "Honey, everyone makes mistakes. The house is fine."

Beck looks up. "My house is on fire?" he asks.

Curiously. Not mad. Just confused.

Despite the alarms still blaring inside.

"No," I tell him.

"Burned to the ground," Ellie sobs.

"It's not—" I start.

"IT WILL BE. Mom. I want to go *home."*

Beck looks at me, shrugs in bewilderment, and then saunters to his sister. "C'mon, Ellie. I got you."

"She's in a bathrobe," I say.

"I'm commando," he offers.

Tucker's still crying. The sirens are getting louder. And when Beck helps Ellie shuffle past us, she doesn't look up when she whispers, "I'm sorry, Wyatt."

Having my arm gnawed off by a bear with dull teeth would be less painful than the searing ache shredding my heart. "Ellie—"

Beck shuts her in the car, and he, too, doesn't look at me as he walks around to the driver's seat. The engine roars back to life, and he pulls out of the driveway thirty seconds before the fire truck screeches to a halt at the house.

"The fire's out," I tell the firefighters, but the words are hollow. "Kitchen accident."

They still file inside.

Mrs. Ryder wraps her arms around both me and Tucker, and I wish I was seven again so I could fucking cry too.

Because it's Ellie.

She's strong. She's smart.

And when she's fucking determined, there's nothing in the world that will stop her.

And she's determined that I'm not good for her.

I grip Tucker tighter, because *fuck*.

One day, he'll grow up and leave me too. And we still have the teenage years to get through, when he'll probably hate me.

"I love her," I whisper to Mrs. Ryder.

"I know, honey," she says softly. "I've always known. She'll come around."

I shake my head, but I don't answer.

Because she won't.

She's made up her mind.

And thirty minutes after I thought I was finally in, finally right, it turns out I'm out.

TWENTY-SEVEN

Wyatt

IT TAKES LESS than an hour for us to get the all-clear to head back inside, but it feels like weeks. Especially with a sleeping Tucker in my arms. He's dead weight once he drifts off.

"Watch those towels," one of the firemen tells me as they depart.

"Yeah. Got it."

I get Tucker put to bed, and I'm about to collapse into my own bed in the next room when I realize I left my phone in the master bedroom downstairs before the fire. On the off-chance Ellie's willing to talk to me, I don't want to miss her. I hit the bottom of the stairs and realize Beck's back.

He's lounging in the living room. Alone.

"Where's Ellie?" I can't help it. The question rolls out.

"Cooper's place."

"*In her bathrobe*?"

"Doesn't really need clothes for sleeping, does she?" He grins at me, like nothing in the fucking world is fucking wrong, and I consider decking him. He might have two inches on me, but I have more muscle.

Plus, hitting something would feel damn good right now.

Maybe.

Probably not.

But it's worth a try.

"Want a beer?" he asks me.

"No." I scrub a hand over my face. "Yes."

"Awesome. What've we got? Smells like toast. You hungry?"

"That's *burnt dish towel.*"

"Eh. Never liked that one anyway." He leads the way into the kitchen, digs into the fridge and emerges with two bottles of Sam Adams. "Ping-pong?"

"You know I've been sleeping with your sister, right?"

"Yep."

"There a reason I'm still standing?"

His blue eyes flicker over me, and for half a second, I think he's going to deck me. "Looks like she already got you."

"She sneezed."

"Son of a *bitch.*" He gets me with a jab to the shoulder. "Keep that shit to yourself."

I recoil. "Fuck, you do that—never mind. Don't want to know."

"Exactly, motherfucker."

He shoves the second beer at me. "Ping-pong. Now."

We troop down to the basement, and he flips on the lights. If I wasn't watching, I wouldn't have noticed him casting a glance at the water stain in the ceiling.

"Didn't mean to break your house," I mutter.

"Fuck, man, it's just a house. I've got more."

In the game room, he claims the far end of the ping-pong table and tosses me a paddle. "Talk."

I set my beer aside and serve a ball.

And while we battle it out for superiority in ping-pong—he's winning, because I have no heart left to put in it—I tell him everything.

Everything.

Starting with Christmas.

He doesn't say anything for three games after I'm done. It's past two in the morning. We're just standing here, hitting a fucking ping-pong ball back and forth, beers gone, the ball hitting the table and our paddles the only sound.

Finally, he tosses his paddle to the table. "You love her?"

Fuck. My chest threatens to cave in. "Yes."

"Huh."

A Beck Ryder *huh* can mean anything from *you're in my seat* to *clogged the toilet again* to *oh, good, meatloaf leftovers.* "*Huh* what?"

He shrugs. "All she'd say was *Tucker needs him alive more than I need to bang him again.* I think you're fucked."

"Thanks. Helpful. Real helpful."

"And Mom's making pancakes in the morning. Told me to tell you to sleep as late as you want, she'll make you more."

I dig the heel of my palms into my eye sockets, because I don't want *pancakes.*

I want Ellie to have some faith that *we can do this.*

But I'm supposed to leave to drive back to Georgia in a few hours, because I go back to work Monday.

"You believe we're cursed?" I ask Beck.

"Nah. Met too many witch doctors over the years. Your case is too boring."

He was always unpredictable even before the boy band days. Now, he's unpredictable with a worldly bent, which is mildly terrifying at times.

"Can you convince Ellie?" I ask.

"You want *me* to convince *my sister* that I know more than she does about something? Dude. It's one thing to say you love her. It's another to act like you don't know her at all."

"The Ellie I know would say fuck the universe."

His smile drops. "Yeah. Fucking Blond Caveman."

I start. "You—"

"Her ex. The douche-nugget."

"Didn't know you called him that too." A thought strikes me, and I squint at him. "Was this your plan when you asked me to annoy her?"

"That you break my dishwasher and burn my house down?"

"To hook me and Ellie up."

"Nah. That was Levi."

I owe another buddy a text. "Levi," I repeat doubtfully.

"After you showed up at the hospital, he said the only other time he's seen that look on a man's face was Tripp, when Jessie had all those complications with delivery."

"You miss the part where it was my fault she was on the road?"

"Oh, go shove your responsibility complex up your ass. You weren't the drunk shitbag who hit her, and you weren't the fuck-weasel who dumped her on Christmas Eve. She made up her mind she wasn't staying at Mom and Dad's that night the minute she saw you, and we both know it. She just wanted to pick a fight, just like you wanted to pick a fight. It was shitty timing, but it wasn't your fault. Got it?"

"Yeah," I mutter.

I don't know if I believe him yet, but I hear him.

Maybe Ellie's right.

Maybe we are safer apart.

TWENTY-EIGHT

Ellie

MY LEG IS POUNDING like a mother, there's an annoying light shining directly at my eyelids, something smells faintly like moldy gym socks, and there's a godawful racket coming from outside the doorway.

Sounds like—

Oh, *dammit*.

Sounds like my brother trying to hit those falsetto notes Levi can reach but Beck most definitely can*not*. He's not *bad*, but they didn't add him to the band for his musical talent.

Nope, they added him for the eye candy.

Blech.

He bursts into the room, and I remember I'm not at his house.

I'm at Cooper Rock's house half a mile up the road. Because Wyatt and I tried to burn down Beck's house last night.

"Is your house still standing?" I ask, realizing I'm croaking like a frog, and also that I don't give two fucks.

The universe spoke.

I listened.

And it hurts like hell.

"Damn straight," he says. "C'mon. Get up. They haven't

found the peg leg yet. I want to go look, but I can't go without a disguise."

"Go buy yourself a peg leg." I shove my head under the pillow, which smells like mothballs, and I really don't care.

Yum, mothballs.

Like death, but mothier.

"You know you broke my best friend's heart."

"Talk to the universe. I'm saving his life." My voice cracks, and I want to hit something, but I also want to roll over and go back to sleep and hope that when I wake up in five or six years, I won't have residual pain in my leg and Wyatt will have found a safe, kind, motherly type of woman that he's madly in love with who gives him blow jobs every night after she bakes cookies for Tucker.

Okay, maybe I'm not willing to go that far. I didn't even get the chance to give him a blow job before fate decided blowing up Beck's house was more important.

Great.

Now I'm dictating when his imaginary girlfriends can go down on him.

And possibly my eyes are leaking.

And if any fucking asshole woman bakes Tucker cookies—

I squeeze my eyes shut, because Tucker's adorable and sweet, but he's not mine.

"Eeeellllliiiiiiieeeeeeeee," Beck whines. "Get uuuuuuuuuppp." He pokes me in the back.

I let him.

He pokes me again.

I still don't move.

When he pokes me the third time, and I *still* don't react, the fucker sits on me. Right on my back with his bony butt.

"Aaahhlp!" I grunt. "Get *off.*"

"I missed my sister," he declares.

"I can't breathe, you ass."

He moves to sit on my calves, and now, even if I wanted to, I don't think I could bend right to punch him. "And what do I come home to? A woman who's not my sister walking around in my sister's body. What did you do with Ellie, Fake Ellie?

Where'd you put her? Are you from Zygorb? Are you an alien wearing my sister's skin?"

"You are annoying as fuck."

"*I'm* annoying? You're the one who's pulling this shitty *woe is me, the universe hates me, and for once in my life I'm gonna just lay down and take it because I'm afraid to love somebody who might actually break my heart* shit."

I freeze.

Because that might be hitting too close to home.

"Go. Away."

"Wyatt's a good dude, Ellie. And he likes you despite you."

"And he flies in airplanes for his day job and we can't even kiss without dishwashers leaking and towels catching on fire and Tucker deserves to grow up with a good dad."

Beck heaves a loud, annoyed sigh and climbs off me. "Fine. Have your pity party. But if you don't get up, I'm calling Monica, and you know she'll skip her honeymoon to be here."

"Dick move. And you'd put her on a private jet and upgrade her to the fanciest cruise in the world to make it up to her."

"Yeah, but she won't know that when she comes running."

Which is why she's my best friend.

My best *girl* friend.

My best *friend* friend might be—*dammit*.

"And I'll send Mom," he adds. "Oh, and by the way, Wyatt was *pissed* when he found out Cooper lives so close. Dude thought he was bicycling up the mountain to deliver you donuts because he's angling to get into your pants. Isn't that a hoot? Ten minutes, Ell. And then I'm singing again too."

He heads out the door whistling like he has fucking sunshine in his sparkly bright soul, and I realize I'm naked.

I'm naked, with a healing black eye, a sore hip and thigh, and a big ol' pile of ash in my chest.

But that's how it has to be.

Because I've hurt enough people in my life.

I won't put Wyatt in danger. He deserves better.

TWENTY-NINE

Ellie

I'D PLANNED to stay in Shipwreck through the weekend for recovery time, but with Beck back, the odds of having a minute of peace are nil. Not because he's always as annoying as he was this morning, but because he'll be calling anyone he can to hang out while he's in town, which will undoubtedly be three days or less.

And I don't want to be in the house when he sees the new high score on Frogger.

Too many memories.

So I convince my dad to ride with me back to Copper Valley before lunch.

When we hit the 256 loop around the city, my eyes sting, because we're officially now out of the country and out of the mountains. It's back to the hustle and bustle. Traffic. Billboards. Skyscrapers.

Dad's quiet the entire ninety-minute drive. When I pull into the driveway of the red brick colonial in the middle-class neighborhood where I grew up, with the old basketball hoop still over the garage door, my eyes burn again.

Dad squeezes my knee. "Been through a lot this year."

He doesn't tell me I'm overreacting. Or that it's okay to be scared, but not okay to let fear rule my life, or any of the other things I logically know.

That's not how Dad works.

Probably because all the rest of us finally talked him into silence over the years.

But he does offer me a scoop of homemade peach cobbler if I want to stay a few hours.

So that's how I find myself curled up on my parents' couch, watching the Fireballs get creamed in high definition, while my dad cuts and sugars early season peaches for our late lunch of peach cobbler.

I don't realize I've drifted off to sleep until the doorbell rings, and when I wake up, I'm disoriented and confused, and it takes me a minute to remember why my heart hurts.

Wyatt.

He probably hates me.

I hope he does. That'll make it easier for him to move on.

I curl tighter into a ball. The game's over, and now an old Meg Ryan and Tom Hanks movie is on.

"Ellie, I'm going for a walk," Dad calls from the front door.

"'Kay," I answer, frog voice and all.

I haven't had any peach cobbler yet, but I should go home. I don't have any food. I need to do laundry. And catch up on work email.

Plus, I could stop at a pet shelter on the way and ask to play with the dogs for a few hours. Guaranteed pick-me-up.

Since Beck sometimes shares my social media posts about dogs that haven't found their forever homes—always with a caption like *Sharing for my sister, who wishes she'd been born a dog so it would be socially acceptable for her to lick my face*—I'm undeservedly welcome at all the shelters in the metro area.

I'm staring blindly at Meg Ryan's profile on the television when the hairs on the back of my neck prickle, and the pile of ashes in my chest gives a big ol' *whomp.*

There's a shadow in the doorway.

A Wyatt-size shadow. Or possibly more than a shadow.

That *whomp* turns into a staccato beat of *whomp* after *whomp* after *whomp*.

"Please," I whisper, and I don't know if I'm asking him to stay or leave. I just know it hurts.

It hurts to think about hurting him.

It hurts to think about losing him.

And it hurts to be terrified that disaster is waiting around every corner if I reject both of my first two options.

He steps slowly into the room, eyes trained on me, searching, asking.

I don't even have to look him in the eye to know.

He's not afraid.

He's not afraid of anything.

"You okay?" he asks, and that voice.

God, I love his voice. Rich and smooth and warm, like hot chocolate after a day playing in the snow.

"Fine," I say hoarsely, and we both know I'm lying.

I can't tell if he's tired, frustrated, or all of the above, but I do know the yellowing bruise on his eye is all the reminder I need of the danger of the two of us getting together.

"Where's Tucker?" I ask, and *dammit*, there's another flame attacking the ashes in my chest.

"With your dad. He's not too happy about the drive coming up."

The drive.

He should've already left.

Instead, he's still here, lowering himself to the couch on the opposite end of where I'm curled up, and it's all I can do not to crawl across the cushions and into his lap to hold him and tell him how sorry I am.

For everything.

For being a shithead when we were kids. For seducing him at Christmas when we were both hurting.

For not answering his phone calls after the accident.

For pushing him away.

"I love you," he says quietly, his voice husky but strong. No hitch. No hesitation. "I've spent my whole life afraid of what it would be like to love you, but I do, Ellie. I love you."

"You shouldn't." He's going to break me.

"I never thought I was built for marriage. I never believed in forever. But I look at you, and I can feel it. I can *see* it. You? You're everything I never knew I wanted. Never knew I *needed*. I didn't believe in forever until I believed in you."

Break me? No. *Destroy* me. "We're—we're *dangerous*, Wyatt."

"If there's anyone in the world who can give the universe a middle finger and tell it to kiss your ass if it thinks it's going to stand in your way, it's you." He sets a piece of paper on the cushion between us. "I don't care if it takes you two hours or forty years. I'll wait. You will *always* be the only woman I'll ever love."

My breath hitches when he takes my hand and kisses my cheek, because *yes*, he's everything I want.

Everything.

But I'm terrified.

My entire life, all I wanted was to meet the goal.

Of course I dated Patrick. He checked all the boxes. Handsome. Successful. Smart.

We could've had a lovely marriage where neither of us actually had to love each other, where there was no danger of a broken heart, because all we wanted was someone to be married to.

But I could have so much more.

Laughter. Joy. Tears. Heartbreak.

With a man who *knows* me. Who *gets* me. Who *accepts* me.

All of me. The good and the bad. The pretty and the ugly. The broken and the whole.

If I'm willing to go for it.

Wyatt doesn't pause on his way out the door.

He doesn't have to.

Because he's tossed the ball back in my court. And left his address, his home phone number, and his work phone number on the couch between us.

It's my turn to decide what to do.

If I'm going to do anything at all.

THIRTY

Wyatt

I FUCKED UP.

I fucked up hardcore. And I hate fucking up.

I also hate hundred-degree weather with humidity so high you can't get your balls dry when you get out of the shower in the morning, but that's life in Georgia.

I hate hearing from my colonel that there's nothing we can do right now to reapply for early release from my service commitment.

I hate that I'd be arrested for being AWOL if I left fucking Georgia forever anyway in August when I have to take Tucker back to Copper Valley.

And I hate that I feel like a shitty parent because I *hurt,* and I don't know if I'm making this the best or the worst summer of my son's life.

"Wow, Dad, you missed that by a mile," he calls with a laugh as I jog after a baseball in my backyard. The live oaks provide enough shade to block the sun from helping the grass grow. Or maybe the grass has also lost the will to live in the fucking heat.

My hand's sweating so bad my glove can barely stay on.

But Tucker's grinning and squealing and laughing while we play catch, which is really more him flinging the ball wildly about the backyard while I try to aim to gently toss a baseball into his mitt.

I love Saturdays.

And I hate Saturdays.

"Does Miss Captain Ellie know how to play catch?" Tucker asks when I toss him the ball.

"Yep."

"Is she as good as you?"

"Don't know, bud."

"Can I see her when I go back with Mom?"

"That's up to your mom."

"Ha! Dad, you missed *again*."

I sure as fuck did.

I bend to grab the ball as my phone rings, and when I see who's calling, I almost drop it.

Both the ball and the phone, actually.

"Hey, bud, I gotta take this," I say. "Throw it at that back tree for a bit, okay? Be right back."

"Okay, Dad!"

I angle around to the side of the two-bedroom brick house I'm renting a couple miles from the base and put the phone to my ear, my heart in my throat. "Ellie?"

"I thought of you while I masturbated last week and then I ran over a squirrel."

My lungs freeze and I grunt out an unintelligible answer.

She barks out a high-pitched laugh. "Kidding. I mean, not about thinking about you while I masturbate. I mean about the squirrel. Nothing bad happened."

"Fuck, Ellie," I manage, because now I'm hard as a pipe and so fucking glad to hear her voice and terrified what she might say next.

"And I've kissed your picture every night this week before I went to bed, and all that happened was I ran out of milk."

Her voice is wobbling, which is understandable, because my knees are wobbling too. "And?" I ask.

"I miss you," she whispers.

"I miss you too."

"Did you know the odds of getting in an accident *and* having your house burn down in the same lifetime are less than your odds of getting struck by lightning?"

I have no idea the real statistics. "Of course. I remember all the Trivial Pursuit answers I read."

She laughs, and it sounds watery, and I wish to fuck I could hold her right now. Or just look at her. "Shut up," she says, but there's none of the old venom or irritation.

This is all playful Ellie.

Hesitantly playful, but playful.

"When I'm right, it's my duty to tell you so." My cheeks crack with the effort of smiling, and my heart's buzzing like it's hooked up to a car battery. But this is what we do.

We give each other shit.

"Fine, Mister Smartypants. What are the odds I'm in your driveway?" she asks.

I freeze.

But only a split second before I'm striding to the front of the house.

The back bumper of a white Prius comes into view.

My pulse amps higher.

She's here.

Ellie's here.

I drop my hands to my side, just staring while she pulls herself out of the driver's seat. She cut her hair shorter, so it's framing her ears with crazy, beautiful curls. Her blue eyes match the deep summer sky, but the hesitancy in them almost makes my knees buckle.

"You drove," I say dumbly.

Her lips hitch toward the sky. "The whole way. After I told the universe I was coming to talk you out of your pants. And no vultures attacked my car. Bears didn't dash in front of me. Random ice storms didn't pop up out of nowhere. My hotel didn't burn down. And so I don't have to interrupt the space-time continuum and bring about another ice age."

I'm supposed to smile, but I still can't believe she's standing here. "What—why—"

She limps as she starts around the car, but holds a hand up when I move toward her. "Do you know what irritates the fuck out of me about you?"

My eyes shift toward the side of the house, but I can hear Tucker still laughing in back, so he missed that little F-bomb. "How perfect I am?" I guess, even though I'm so fucking far from it.

"Exactly. You even knew I was going to say that."

Her gait is smoothing out as she rounds the car.

My fingers itch, and my arms are aching to hold her, but I wait, because I know she'll read me the riot act if I try to make this any easier on her.

"I'm not perfect, Ellie."

"Do you remember what you said? That if anyone would flip off the universe and do what I wanted anyway, it was me?"

She stops inches from me, the waver still in her voice.

I nod.

"You forgot a part."

"What part?"

"The part where I won't have to do it alone."

"I thought that's what you were afraid of."

"I don't want to be afraid to live."

"That's my girl."

"I love you, Wyatt." She finally closes the distance between us and lines her body up with mine, her hands sliding up my chest. "Do you still want me?" she whispers.

"Always."

"Even if *always* is only like thirty more seconds?"

I laugh, because she's teasing. And she's *here*. "Ellie Ryder, I will love you long after my heart stops beating. And *that*, you can count on."

She pushes up on her toes while I angle my head down to meet her, and there's no head-crashing, no black eyes, no sneezes, just her lips teasing mine, *here*, real, *here*, in the hot fucking Georgia sauna, her hands exploring while I crush her to me because I am *never* letting her go.

Ever.

"Dad! Are you—*Miss Captain Ellie!*"

The joy in Tucker's voice puts a lump in my throat, and I'm blinking hard as Ellie pulls back and leans down to hug my son. "Hey, kiddo. You teaching your dad to play ball?"

"Yeah, he's kinda bad. He keeps missing the ball. Are you better?"

"Probably not."

"That's okay. We have ice cream when you're bad."

I choke on a laugh. "We *what*?"

He grins hopefully at me. "Right, Dad? Ice cream. Miss Captain Ellie, can you stay for ice cream? My dad's grilling burgers later too. You can have his. He'll go to the store for more."

I gape at him, because he's moving in and pulling smoother moves than I have.

But Ellie hugs him again. "You are adorable."

"I don't think he needs encouragement," I tell her.

She rises and smiles at me, but as she does, something white lands in her hair.

My jaw slips.

Her brows furrow, and she starts to reach for her head, but I snag her hand. "Don't. Just... Hey, Tucker? Go get the gloves and bring them inside, okay? We'll get ice cream. We'll get ice cream right now."

He giggles. "Miss Captain Ellie, a bird just pooped in your hair!"

"Go on," I say, giving him a gentle shove in the right direction.

"Are you *kidding* me?" Ellie mutters.

I can't decide if I want to laugh or if I need to go into full-on overprotective mode, but as soon as Tucker turns his back, she lifts a middle finger to the sky. "Bring it, asshole," she mutters.

"If you really meant it," I tell her, "you'd use both middle fingers."

Something squawks, and a bird bounces off the neighbor's side window. It falls on the ground, leaps to its feet, bounces around like it's dizzy for a minute, and then takes off again in the opposite direction.

Ellie dusts her hands. "That's right. Who's in charge now?"

I don't bother stifling a smile.

Because that's my girl.

EPILOGUE

Wyatt, who most definitely put a ring on it a year later in a story for another time

THERE'S nothing quite as beautiful as watching Ellie pause in her yoga routine next to the bar in Beck's basement to smile at her ring. Tucker's passed out cold upstairs after more fun at the pirate festival than even I thought possible, and though he'll be up with the sun, I have plans for this pretty lady that involve getting her naked ASAP and neither of us sleeping for hours.

"That as far as you can stretch?" I ask. "C'mon, Ryder. You're barely touching your knees."

She rolls her eyes, but she's still smiling. "With my nose, you big jerk. Like to see you try."

I settle on the ground next to her, on my hands and knees, and I bend over and kiss her knee. "See? Nothing to it."

"You goober," she says with a laugh, rubbing my short hair and catching me by the back of the neck so she can kiss me.

And so I can kiss her back.

If I live to be two hundred, I'll never get tired of kissing Ellie. I sometimes can't believe I spent so many years thinking she was just an annoying twit, because *this* Ellie is all heart.

And too many people overlook it because she's also determination and grit and honesty. But it's all driven by that heart that she puts into everything.

She pushes me onto my back and straddles me. "Have I told you how much I love my rings?" she whispers, because yep, she got more than one.

"Nope. I'm pretty sure you hate them and you're just humoring us."

She laughs. "You're absolutely correct. But since they come with Tucker, I guess I'll keep them." Her hair tickles my cheeks as she bends to kiss me, and I thread my fingers through the soft, curly locks while I tease her tongue with mine.

Her phone buzzes on the floor next to us, but we both ignore it. Her fingers are trailing over the vacation stubble on my jaw, and there's nothing I love more than her touch on my face.

Except maybe the way she's rocking her pussy over my rapidly hardening cock.

That's pretty fucking amazing too.

Especially knowing how hard she's worked to get so much strength and range of motion back in her leg.

Anytime Beck gives me shit for sleeping with his sister, I point out how much I've improved her flexibility.

Her phone buzzes again. "Sorry," she murmurs. "Couldn't help myself. I posted a picture of my rings on Twitter."

"So you *do* like them."

"Maybe a little." Her eyes sparkle while she dips her head to press a kiss to my neck. I slide my hands under her shirt, and —"*Dammit*, Ellie, I fucking hate your sports bras."

She laughs while she straightens and pulls off both her shirt *and* the stupidly tight rubber band with straps that require flexibility and acrobatics to pull off.

I don't mind the show, but it looks like wearing it would hurt.

Though I do like the way her breasts just somehow fall right into my waiting palms while she's still wrangling the thing over her head.

So soft. And those gorgeous pink tips that harden immediately under my thumbs are making my cock ache. I lean up to take one in my mouth, and she gasps and grips my shoulders. "*Wyatt*."

"Mmm," I hum against her nipple, and her breath catches again while she arches into me.

Her phone erupts in a series of buzzes, and she laughs breathlessly. "I should shut that off."

"Ignore it," I reply, shifting my focus to her other breast while I roll her wet nipple between my thumb and finger.

"Oh, god, Wyatt, what if Tucker gets up again?" she whispers.

"I'll hear him."

"Like last time?"

"Ellie. He's passed out cold." I blow on her nipple, and it works.

She moans and grabs my face and kisses me hard, then orders me to lose my shirt too.

I'm happily obliging when her phone blows up.

Not like kitchen-fire-level blowing up, but a steady stream of buzzes that just don't stop.

At all.

She huffs and leans over to grab it. "Stupid pho—oh."

Her eyes go wide.

Then wider.

Her mouth follows suit.

"Wyatt," she whispers.

That raging hard ache in my cock disappears, because something's wrong.

Something's *seriously* fucking wrong.

"What? What is it?"

"Beck—" she starts.

My veins freeze over. For all the shit I've given him, if something happened to Beck—

"No, no," she says quickly. "He's okay. He's okay. But—the jokes. The pranks. His mouth. He—"

She cuts herself off and holds her phone in front of my face.

I read the first text from Monica.

Another from her mom.

One's come in from Levi, and I realize if I had my phone on me, it would probably be blowing up too, but my phone's upstairs.

And then there's the picture.

The picture of a tweet.

Sent by Beck.

Looks like something he'd say to Ellie, but he most definitely did *not* send that Tweet to his sister.

"He's fucking dead," I say, my own eyeballs like saucers.

"His career is," she whispers back.

We make eye contact.

"Surprise engagement party tomorrow night at home," I croak out. "He's coming."

She's off me in a heartbeat, putting her phone to her ear, undoubtedly calling the dumbass. "He's home?" she asks me while I hear his voicemail pick up.

"Flying in overnight."

I'm on my feet now too.

I don't care how much shit he gives me for dating his sister—or how many other pranks he's pulled on me this past year alone—he's my brother.

And he just made the mistake of his life.

"I'll start packing," I say while I throw on my shirt.

She leaves her sports bra on the ground and struggles into her tank top. "I'm calling Mom and Dad."

"Tucker can sleep in the car."

She winces. "But the festival—"

"Ellie."

She studies me a minute, then nods.

Would I rather spend the night making her moan my name?

Fuck, yes.

But family comes first. And if the way Ellie's phone is blowing up all over again is any indication, family needs her right now.

And me.

And every last one of the guys from the neighborhood.

For what Beck just did, he's going to need all the support he can get.

"Ellie?" I say softly while I trail her up the stairs.

"What?"

"You know this isn't because we got engaged, right? We don't actually cause disasters."

She pauses to look at me, and then we both laugh. Except neither one of us actually thinks it's funny.

We're loading up the car before she says any more about it. Tucker's objecting to being strapped into his booster seat in the middle of the night, and Ellie's about to climb in to sit next to him and snuggle him as best she can in the car when she turns to look at me.

"We really are cursed," she says slowly, but then a smile pops out. "But there's no one in the world I'd rather be cursed with."

AMERICA'S GEEKHEART SNEAK PEEK

*If you love hot, sexy Hollywood men, Tweets gone terribly wrong, and charmingly adorable heroines looking for where they fit in the world, read on for an unedited excerpt of **America's Geekheart**!*

Beckett Ryder, aka a man completely oblivious that he's just mistweeted his way to being public enemy number one

Life is pretty fucking perfect.

Weather's a glorious seventy-five degrees and sunny on this brilliant June morning. My new jogging shoes fit like I'm running on a cloud. That green leafy canopy over Reynolds Park is hitting that perfect level of shade, and I've got my tunes dialed up and nowhere to be until the engagement party for my sister tonight.

Ten solid hours of doing whatever the fuck I want.

I'm grinning to myself as I run the familiar pathway through the city park, so fucking glad to be back in Copper Valley. Love my job, but there is no place in the world like home.

I nod to a woman pushing a jogging stroller going the other way, and she scowls and flips me off.

Odd.

Crazies are normal when I'm in LA, or sometimes in Europe, but here?

My hometown *loves* me.

I dial down the volume on my tunes and double-check my shirt.

Nope, nothing offensive about a Fireballs T-shirt. They might be the biggest losers in baseball, but they're lovable losers.

I glance lower, and—yep, remembered to put pants on today.

I might've been singing along to Levi's latest hit, but I'm not *that* bad. Sure, I was the eye candy in the boy band Bro Code back in the day, but I can still carry a tune.

She must've mistaken me for someone else. Or her fingers are stuck that way. Resting bitch face knows no boundaries. Probably not her fault.

I keep on truckin', and an elderly woman on a bench shakes her cane at me and says something I don't catch while her dog yaps along. I pop out one earbud.

"You're a disgrace to good men everywhere," she crows.

I slow and face her, jogging in place. "Ma'am?"

"Your poor momma must be ashamed."

Ah. The underwear police. Not so unusual. While Levi went on to be a pop sensation when we called it quits as Bro Code, Cash took off for Hollywood, Tripp hung up his fame and settled down, and Davis went into hiding, I took my own route.

My post-boy-band career choices have been known to raise a few eyebrows.

"Yes, ma'am. She's horrified. Y'all have a nice day now." I salute her and head back down the path toward the fountain at the center of the park.

In the years since I first started modeling underwear for Giovanni & Valentino before I branched out into creating a fashion empire of my own, I've had my share of haters. Goes with the business.

But my *momma* isn't ashamed of me.

No more than she was during my boy band days. If anything, she's amused. Resigned, but amused.

Ellie—my sister—gives me trouble. So do all the guys we grew up with.

That's why I love them.

They keep me grounded.

Hell, half of them needed the grounding themselves.

The path curves, and there she is.

My fountain.

Okay, fine, she's not *mine*. But she's on the city's crest, and she just says *home* to me.

I fucking love home, but running the Beck Ryder fashion empire—yeah, go ahead and snort, it's funny—keeps me away a lot.

I burst out into the sunshine and make the loop around the curved sidewalk, feet pounding the concrete, mist brushing my face, the five stone dolphins around the fountain joyfully spitting water into the stone mermaids' buckets on the second tier while a circle of seahorses blows water horns.

The early summer breeze rustles the birch and sugar maple leaves shimmering in the sunlight. The air's clear, the sky my favorite blue. Flowers explode in reds and yellows and purples in the carefully cultivated landscaping that masks the downtown skyscrapers and mutes the noise of the city.

It's my own private welcome home party from nature.

Can't wait to be here more often.

Soon. *So* soon.

I circle the fountain and head back toward the path that leads to the Shuler building and my penthouse at the edge of the park. Tomorrow, I have to get back to work on the surprise I'm announcing for my parents next weekend, plus the final details on selling off my empire, but today, my staff has the day off, my phone's still on airplane mode, and the whole Copper Valley metro area is my oyster.

No phone, no work, no responsibilities.

Maybe I'll leave the city behind and head up into the Blue Ridge mountains for a hike. Nap up there in the fresh air. Get back in time for Ellie and Wyatt's surprise engagement party.

Rumor has it they're serving barbecue.

I haven't had good barbecue in months.

I'm so busy drooling over the thought of real Southern pulled pork that I almost miss the yoga class.

By itself, a yoga class on the lawn by the fountain isn't unusual. But this yoga class seems less into the Namaste and more into hurtling their yoga bricks.

Specifically, at me.

They charge me as a group, a yoga-pants-clad mob racing over the hilly green grass, shouting obscenities and shaking fists. One lady has her mat rolled into a cylinder and is leading the pack *Braveheart* style.

"*Creep!*"

"*Jerk!*"

"*You* go home and get your own damn apron!"

My pulse amps into sprint territory.

"Hey, hey." I hold my hands up in surrender while I jog backwards, because seriously, *what the fuck*? "Y'all know I love you. What's—"

A shoe hurtles at my face. Another yoga brick clips my shoulder.

"Get him, ladies," the *Braveheart* lady yelled.

Oh, *shit*.

They want blood.

I don't have a fucking clue what I did, but these ladies want blood. *My* blood.

My run morphs into a sprint, but for once, my brain's spinning faster than my legs.

The mother and her stroller and her middle finger. The grandmother and her cane. And now a yoga class.

I'm outnumbered.

Probably outsmarted and outmaneuvered too.

Another yoga brick.

And I'm still a mile from safety.

"*Shut up and let your underwear do the talking!*" A clump of— oh, man, that's disgusting. Flying horse poop. Awesome.

I pump my legs harder. Knees higher. Like I'm gonna beat Usain Bolt. Running. *Sprinting*. Away from a mob of angry women.

This is new.

As is having a mob of angry women gaining on me.

The ladies usually love me.

Maybe a run wasn't the best cure for jetlag.

But how was I supposed to know today's International Beck Ryder Is The Enemy Day?

"I'll show you where *you* belong," one of the women screeches.

I don't have a clue where she thinks I belong, or why she thinks I belong there, but I know one thing.

I am totally fucked.

ABOUT THE AUTHOR

Pippa Grant is a stay-at-home mom and housewife who loves to escape into sexy, funny stories way more than she likes perpetually cleaning toothpaste out of sinks and off toilet handles. When she's not reading, writing, sleeping, or trying to prepare her adorable demon spawn to be productive members of society, she's fantasizing about chocolate chip cookies.

Find Pippa at...
www.pippagrant.com
pippa@pippagrant.com

COPYRIGHT

9 781940 517483